Open Couplets

Open Couplets

A Novel

TORSA GHOSAL

YODAPRESS

YODA PRESS
79 Gulmohar Enclave
New Delhi 110 049
www.yodapress.co.in

ISBN 978-93-82579-22-9

Editors in charge: Arpita Das and Lourdes M. Supriya
Typeset in Adobe Caslon Pro, 11/14
By Jojy Philip
Printed at Saurabh Printers Pvt. Ltd.
Published by Arpita Das for YODA PRESS

Prologue

Tuesday, 4 November 2014
9:28 PM

from: Ira Chatterjee <ira.chatterjee12@h-mail.com>
to: Amber Perez <amberscrawls@h-mail.com>

My laryngopharynx burns. Not midnight yet. Fireballs in pint glasses, waiting to be gulped, sit on the kitchen counter. It is last year. We take our grads-can-have-fun maxim to heart. You're drunk enough to rap with such gusto that the lyrics—the wife beating, slut calling, shrew taming gems—shred to pieces. You've done it, Amby; graduated with a Masters in Fine Arts, despite everything. Your daughter must have been a deep sleeper to make it through the night, nestled in the basement. Noises travel far. Walls are thin here. When I lie there at night nowadays, I hear the neighborhood kids yapping away.

Conversations at the Stress Resilience Clinic do me no good. I don't meet people worth talking to any more. Counting the number of days since the last time when I talked to a real person puts me to sleep. I dream of walking amid mirrors, holding on to a string. I have called home more times in the last eight months than in the rest of the three years combined…lol. This is not how it was supposed to be in this Midwestern la-la-land. At any other time I would have gladly taken you up on the invitation to bask in the California sun. But all I can think of is the well. No splash of water, no sound. Did it even happen? At the very least I need to find it. I need to go. The same things happen here day to day. I'm expected to churn out page after page of new knowledge by the given deadlines from an apartment full of junk. Mike's keurig brewer, Xian's TV, your couch. And that after I have taken down all the decorations.

Even in our department there are such few old faces, apart from the faculty, of course. Speaking of which, Dr Harris has been very accommodating. If I had any other advisor, I would have quit by this point. She reminds me of the responsibility I have toward the people whose stories I bear. I have considered leaving the recordings and transcripts in an archive for someone more sorted. What was I thinking when I started this project? Nothing of any consequence can come out of my dissertation. If I defend it, it will only entail rushed revisions and publication because in five years this state university, which technically owns my doctoral research, will make it public anyway. Basically, I'll have to beat them to it. But Dr Harris will not let me go. She believes I am too close to the finish line to give up. Perhaps she does not want her advisee to bump up the already high attrition rate. So, she agreed to let me visit India. She believes I will be back by January.

Things depend on how long it takes to locate Zaidi. I am not coming back without him and I don't buy Riz's far fetched story. And what if the story is true? Zaidi always said that stories have holes for us to enter and change their course.

Wasn't everything about Zaidi a story? His poems had plots, his e-mails were histories, and living with him was another story whose absurd climax I am trying to parse. I revisit every turn the story took, search every locale, but memories and messages can take me only so far. I am flying out this weekend. Will try to be in touch.

Cheers,
Ira

1

Wet clay weighs the damp air down, competing with the hard sun's sultriness. Earlier, a crow collapsed on the balcony. A coterie of mourners in black took charge of the morning's sound-scape. It is nobody's business to interrupt their incessant cawing. If you do not like the sound, you can always shut your wooden doors and hope for the best. That's what she did. Now the crow and its companions have disappeared. How far can they go? They must be in the thickets, here, out of sight.

As usual, the balcony rattles just a little with the dawdling freight wagons. Behind that passing train, the daily bathers take another dip in the Hooghly. Quick fingers of a fettler scrape the glaze off the arms of a Kartik idol. A neatly pleated gold-embroidered blue *dhoti* flutters impatiently next to the naked, half-painted model. Nowadays Kartik, the pretty god, commands attention only after the larger orders for Kali and Jagadhatri pujas are complete. She was in *Ma*'s womb when a Kartik idol entered their house for the last time. It is not as if her parents did not want a daughter—they only wanted to honour the family tradition of asking Kartik to bless the pregnant mother with a son. Somewhere, bamboo sticks shake when wire corsets are tightened. What idol are they binding the straw for at this time of the year?—after Kartik, the next one, as far as she can tell, will be Saraswati. But that is months away.

Coat the *rohu* fish with batter. The pink and silver stomach of the fish shines against the blackened brass bowl. The eyes of the rohu taught her what it is to feel pity. Lingering traces of turmeric and the scent of onion-garlic paste emanate from her fingers and yet another drop of oil darkens the green paint of the kitchen wall. Knead the dough, like it is soft clay freshly scooped from the muddy Hooghly. Will it rain this sweltering morning? The rohu is taking on a caramel shade. Let it simmer in the mustard oil.

She leans over the balcony. The alley downstairs is emptier than it has been in the past few months. Durga, Kali, and their entourage have returned to Hooghly as clay and have been subsequently fished out of water as straw and bamboo skeletons. Her craned neck hurts. Collecting the end of her yellow cotton saree, she turns to go inside. A pair of eyes looking up her left shoulder startles her.

In these lanes there is no respite from eyes. No matter what time it is and who you are. This time, though, it is only the pair of Dakini-Yogini models which did not sell during the Kali Puja season. Removed from *Baba's* workshop for the lack of space, the pair guards the porch downstairs. Toward the wee hours of the morning on the day of Kali Puja, Baba was ready to sell those off at practically no cost. Of course, Dakini-Yogini should not even be compared to the star gods like Durga, Kali, Shiva, or even Dhere Gopal. Even the idols with a more humble following, like Manasa, are way above the league of these ugly blue and green ghosts that accompany Kali to the *pandals*; their chief responsibility is to evoke the morbidity of cemeteries. The seasonal function requires an annual, limited supply. By the time Baba realised that his workshop had more pairs of Dakini-Yoginis than he could sell, it was too late. No pandals wanted these even as gifts. Too many Dakini-Yoginis would disturb the fine balance between cultivated morbidity and routine ridiculousness. The best these models can do now is to hold up until the next season.

In the dark, how many times has she mistaken their eye sockets fitted with light bulbs for people! She is not terrified when rows of such blue and green bodies occupy the alleys through the interim period, between Durga and Kali pujas, with their tongues sticking out and eye-bulbs twinkling. This year's idols look like the last year's and last year's looked like the year before. More or less. If you grew up in these Kumartuli lanes, you too would learn to live with the images of gods and ghosts alike. She used to make faces at the Dakini-Yogini. Their parched tongues thirsty for the blood dripping from the neatly butchered heads that they hold in their fist and wear as garlands, mimicking Kali, is a commonplace sight. Kali, being the protagonist of the show, gets to have the more supple and plumper heads around her neck—sometimes her full breasts are sandwiched between handsome butchered heads. Why does blood embellishing the rim of these severed heads look like frills? When heads are sliced off at the neck, where do the bones of the neck go? Do they remain with the headless body—jutting out like fish bones?

Burnt oil. Burnt fish! A crow swoops past the balcony to snatch an uncooked piece of fish from the bowl. She feels the morning slipping between her fingers and licks her palms. No one else will know the taste of raw spices mixed with her sweat. She looks over the balcony to the porch again.

Bells are ringing in the other room. Ma must have filled the little brass cups with Ganges water for the gods to drink.

She used to fancy stealing those cups for playing *ranna-bari*. The clay dolls she sculpted with her own hands required cups of exactly that size but Baba would never get those for her. The utensils she got to play with were always pink, blue, and yellow plastic ones—as useless as Saturdays. The thick and blunt smoke from the deep skillet lacks the sharp twirls of incense smoke rising in that prayer room, drawing shapes in the air before vanishing. And the cloying sweetness of *prasad* invites her. Having touched fish, she can not enter the prayer room without bathing. Wait for Ma to bring the sweets. But first, let the air swell with the resounding vibrations of Ma's conch.

The conch never sounds the same when she blows into it. During Durga Puja, Ma makes sure to compete with the other neighbourhood ladies in an event, organised by the local club, where the one who blows the conch for the longest wins. Ma times herself while practising annually on the eve of the competition. Didn't Ma win this silver-coloured plastic tray a few years back? Silver has blackened, especially on the edges, but the tray is still pretty. Royal. She, on her part, has never managed to even make it to the second round of the competition. In the last couple of years, she has stopped trying. This year, though, she stood first in the sit and draw competition.

Unable to think of anything to draw, she started to sketch the face of a man who was hovering around the place, where she and the other participants were seated. She did not know who this man was, what he was doing there, but his face was strange. He had a mole on the left side of his nose that looked like a black stud. Funny. She could not get the features of his face right and not knowing who he was, did not want her sketch to betray the resemblance. Once this man was in the foreground, she only needed to fill the background to make sure that the face did not look like it was floating in the plain yogurt of the white page. In her school there used to be a drawing class in which the teacher told the students to sketch while he kept himself busy, smoking cigarettes and reading newspapers. Only now and then he would check their last week's or last month's work and even less frequently would he part with any advice pertaining to drawing or colouring. For all practical purposes, the class was a 'free period' and most girls treated it as such. She was also no different but sometimes she did doodle.

She drew one half of a tree trunk and branches in the background, shading with dark brown and navy blue crayons. The rest of the paper could be filled with sky blue. Pencil strokes lining the branches looked like the lines on the man's face in her portrait. She added a few more similar strokes. Make sure the judges also notice that likeness. The pattern would mean something, even though she could not quite fathom exactly what. And then in the evening she found her painting hung on a nylon thread outside the local club alongside some other paintings. These were winners of the competition. Ma and she got their prizes from a person of some significance—that's all that she remembers. Maybe he was the local politician who won the latest election. Or was he the one who lost? She had touched his feet because he looked important.

When Baba and her brother return from the workshop, will she serve them burnt fish? Does she know how expensive fish is? How did the crows manage to snatch fish off the kitchen if she was standing guard? She is *alakhshmi*—a woman who, unlike the goddess Lakshmi, proves detrimental to the smooth functioning of a household. Ma had suspected as much from the loud noise she makes while she walks, the manner in which she scatters rice around her plate while she

eats, and now there remains no doubt at all. Through the
week she does nothing at home on the pretext of going to
school and on Saturdays, when she gets the opportunity to be
of some help, her only contribution is to increase Ma's work.
Now what is to be done with the fish?

Thank god lunches don't last forever. Nor do Ma's
diatribes. So, she can keep her ears attuned to the calls of
the cola man, just in case he happens to pass by, carrying
narrow succulent plastic packs of orange and brown juices.
The *kulfi* cart has stopped coming. When winter is on its
way, she should not crave cold desserts.

One of those hot days that turn into evenings wrapped in
shawl and you crave roasted peanuts and puffed rice daubed
with mustard oil, with a slice of coconut on the side. But it
is time to carry empty buckets downstairs and queue up for
water at the municipal corporation's tap on the street. If she
does not take her place in the queue now, she might not get
water and then, at night, there might be no water for washing
in the toilet or drinking. In any case, all she has to do is stand
in the queue and wait for her brother. He will carry the heavy
buckets filled with water upstairs.

At this queue you meet people you don't want to
meet. Stories from the entire neighborhood float in the air
while windows frame rectangular images to hang in the gallery
of the approaching night. Whispers and hoots collide with the
metallic handles of the buckets. Machines from the nearby
gunjee factories never stop humming. A quarrel breaks out. Of
course it subsides, it always subsides. And here comes Bhola.

A brown cloth tied around his neck like a bib, Bhola
shakes his head vigorously as he approaches the queue. He
is taller than everyone and older than her. She can not think
of a time when Bhola's face looked any different from what

it looks like now. And she can not remember if she has ever
seen Bhola without the bib that absorbs the saliva dripping
from his mouth. Bhola knows everyone here, including her, but
he can not exchange pleasantries. He only makes noises that
range from a deep hoom to shrill shrieks. Bhola shrieked the
loudest when his father arrived on the shoulders of other men
on the tenth day of the Durga Puja this year. Bhola's father was
volunteering with the local club during the ritual immersion
of the Durga idol. He was holding the bamboo and clay base
of the idol, along with six others. As vermillion and pink gulal
coloured the annual slogan, "*Bolo Durga Mai ki joi*," his feet
slipped on the steps of the *ghat*. The ten-feet tall idol landed
on the ground with a thud. It was a few moments before he
realised that his right foot was caught beneath the *pratima*. She
saw it all. She always went to watch the immersion of idols on
the tenth day of the puja, before going to her aunt's house to
seek blessings on the occasion of Bijoya. Coconut *laddoos*!

Somebody else from his family will soon come to replace
Bhola. Everybody knows that if it were left to him, his family
would not get water. She counts the number of buckets ahead
of her. The Chatterjees have sent thirteen tumblers with their
three servants. What do the Chatterjees do with so much
water? Even in the morning when water comes to the tap,
their servants stand ahead of everyone with several buckets.
She knows that young maidservant of theirs. In fact, everyone
knows about that maid: that young girl had washed her face
with the bleaching powder the Chatterjees use to clean their
toilet, in the hope of lightening her complexion. The maid
wanted to resemble the youngest daughter of the Chatterjees,
the well-known beauty whose cheeks were the colour of rose
milk. Come to think of it, even the Durga idol has rose milk
cheeks. Does not everyone crave rose milk cheeks? She can

not even envisage how the young girl endured the burns on her skin. The strong, obnoxious smell coming off the bleaching powder's container induces cough. What had it felt like to press that harsh powder on the forehead, around the eyes, and the nose? Now what makes Bhola laugh? One of his laughter fits, it seems. Years later when she will come to visit her mother from her in-laws' house in another part of the city, she will learn of Bhola's death, his neck sliced off and quashed on the Circular rail track. Bhola stops laughing.

Ma rolls cotton balls, dips them in the mustard oil, and lights them to dispatch evening greetings to the gods. Soon Ma will leave to catch up with her aunt. She will have to get some school home-work done before she can join Ma at her aunt's place. She does not like her cousins as much as she likes her aunt, and that too because her aunt is the best story teller she knows. Much older than Baba-Ma, Aunt has her bouquet of tales ready all day every day. The subject matter could be anything: the gist of the latest film she watched; the girl next door whom she saw communicate in gestures with a guy on a terrace five houses away; the stealth in the ration shop and the soaring price of kerosene; the taste of fish and the culinary skills of women in East Bengal, from where their family came to Kumartuli during partition. Aunt's stories about the other Bengal delight her the most. The terrains, the houses, the lives seem so familiar—only better, more well-off. She hears of the manner in which her grandparents had to leave their old house and workshops in Faridpur. The relatives who remained over there have long given up the idol-making business. The details with which her aunt embellishes this familial history keep changing. How is it that everything of worth having disappeared into thin air makes for the most gorgeous, tellable plots.

She hates it when aunt and Ma ask her to go play Ludo with the cousins. Aunt and Ma's adult heart-to-heart conversation will focus on Baba's and Uncle's irresponsible dealings, their apathy toward their wives' and families' everyday lives. How much the men owe and to whom will be reiterated. Her uncle's business of Sholapith jewellery for the idols is not doing any better than Baba's idol trade. Baba and Uncle refuse to branch out. These days everyone works with more than one material. Artists not only create clay idols but also make other kinds of sculptures with cement, plaster, bronze. But Baba is stuck in clay and Uncle in Sholapith. Last year Baba even refused commissions for a huge plaster Ganesha model for a Marwari function. This is no way to conduct a business, especially when you have mouths to feed.

Her brother joins the queue for water, complaining about Baba. Baba holds him back at the workshop even when there is no real work. The off-season has begun but Baba refuses to go easy on him. Now that he is here, he is not going back to the workshop. He is hungry as well. So he will go home straight away. When Baba comes, he will think of an explanation. Which essentially means that tonight around dinner time there will be a tiff between her brother and Baba, in which Baba will attempt to convince her brother about the importance of knowing the idol-making craft inside out for sustaining the family business. Someone in the family ought to carry on what the forefathers practised, so that the craft continues to thrive. Her brother, on his part, will remind Baba, without mincing words, that the craft is not really thriving. Her brother will then dramatically rise from the dinner table and venture out, having finished most of the dinner. Only a few morsels will be left on his plate to give Ma adequate cues for chiding Baba: no respite for the only son of the house even during dinner.

When Baba and his son are not at loggerheads, their takes on the state of the art are much more aligned. For years the Bengal government has promised artisans and workshop-owners better working and living conditions. Some of the city's administrators even waxed eloquent about soon-to-be-built art galleries for the artisans to display permanent exhibits. Connoisseurs from London, Germany, and America would supposedly visit, appreciate, and buy from those galleries. Great publicity opportunity—after all, the world should recognise the talent of our indigenous artisans. Nothing materialised. Baba says this craft is one of devotion. But who can work devotedly when there is filth around? The business itself is seasonal. Baba invests in acquiring raw materials and hiring skilled labour, from rural Bengal, Bihar and Orissa, months before he can sell the idols. Some idols are commissioned but in the case of smaller pujas like Vishwakarma, Kartik, or Saraswati, idols must be prepared in advance. On the day of the puja the models are arranged in rows for customers to choose. Baba has been lucky in that his relatives—like his sister's husband and other second cousins—chip in whenever he requires loans. Of course Baba helps them out whenever he can, though such occasions are becoming increasingly less frequent. Though Baba rarely acknowledges it, doubts simmered in his heart when he let his son drop out of school to apprentice in his workshop. When the business passes on to the next generation it will be in worse shape. Maybe he is not leaving his son a rich family legacy but one that will ensure his impoverished survival.

Her brother will not appear anywhere close to their house before late night when his friends—men who are closer to Baba's age than her brother's— will find a spot on their porch, sit on a tarpaulin sheet, and deal cards to play. Baba's only solace is that her brother is at least not killing and bombing, unlike the other boys his age. Many of those boys, who frequent the local club, are undercover rebels. It is not uncommon to wake up to the sound of explosions these days. She often tried to picture these rebel boys. Would they be fierce? Finally, during a police raid, two of them sought asylum in their house. Ma let them hide in her bedroom and warded off the police from the door. She felt proud of her Ma.

Who clears his throat right next to the window this late at night? Also, belching and spitting?—will certainly stain the porch. The intolerable stench of cigarette and liquor will announce the return of the son close to midnight. He will act up before Ma but his drunkenness will subside once he enters the bedroom he shares with his sister. From his sister he will learn what transpired between Ma and Baba once he left. The laughter of the men downstairs will remain faintly audible. They will still be at the game that her brother lost.

The dew settles on the rusty grill of the window. She was standing right there, holding the window's grills, when a man—a foreigner as far as she could tell, having seen too many of them in these lanes around puja—clicked her photograph. They come to see how the artisans craft such huge models in these small and dirty workshops of Kumartuli. Of course, there must be great artists in their far off countries but they have the space and time to sculpt. Here Baba sculpts models that reach up to the ceiling of the room in which he works. Even with his eyes closed Baba can draw the eyes of the goddess. She ran downstairs to ask the photographer the name of the paper in which her photo will appear. But by the time she reached, the man was clicking children who were playing with marbles on the street. Talking to him would be awkward. Maybe her photo was printed somewhere, in some other country. Maybe not.

The fettler re-appears when she closes her eyes. He holds a brush and a small knife. His fingers are the colour of clay. The face of a Durga idol lies on a stone slab. Next to the fettler there is a row of medium-sized headless straw models pushing against each other. The models are kicking one another for space. With the back of the brush he draws the hairline of the model at hand and keeps brushing along that line until the curve is distinct. No excess clay remains. He dips his thumb in a bowl of water and repeats the gesture along the hairline with his thumb. All the while the model's face stares at him, its eyes without eye balls. The back of the model's face is dark and hollow. The fettler lifts his head to catch a glimpse of the fast graying sky. Drains will swell with the straw that the rain shears off the models and splatters of clay will chart the edges of the narrow street. Cover the models with tarpaulin, fast. A spray of water cools the fettler's forehead. The model's eyes glare as the droplets infuse them with sight. The black mole on the fettler's nose glistens. His face turns toward her. His face turns into her face.

2

Search: *Home*
Monday, 10 December 2012
6:37 PM

from: ira.chatterjee12@h-mail.com
to: Fasahat Zaidi <zaidi.fasahat@h-mail.com>

Heylo Z,
Reached *home* on schedule but even the 3 hours layover in
Delhi was not enough. I was all set to miss the connection
to Kolkata lol. It was my puppy face in the security line that
clinched it for me :-D. Btw, that swanky Terminal 3 has its
problems—no free WiFi. To purchase a few hours' connection,
you need an Indian cellphone number. Imagine! And I hate to
tell you but you were right about my choice of flights. Flying
all the way to San Francisco, before coming to DC, and then
onward to Europe in order to save $$$ was not so wise. I did
have Amber and Clara for company till SFO and they waited
out with me, which was great though all Amber did was flip
through a daycare brochure. And Clara did not cry on the
plane. I hate children crying on planes as much as I hate
sitting next to passengers who throw up while flying. SFO

has great places to eat, unlike our la-la-land airport, and we barged into the snobby business class lounge to click a selfie with a miniature plane that had caught Clara's eyes. You'll see it's a cool airport when you go there later this month but oh god oh god, an aerial tour of North America isn't such a good add-on to the long journey *home*.

I hope you are missing me already and you are starving for words to drop from the tip of my fingers onto your tongue. Because, I have until dinner and this is going to be a long e-mail. And you've got to read through :). Mom's making something in the kitchen. I smell fried onions and garlic. To get dinner without cooking is bliss, right? Okay, maybe not so much for you 'cos you love to serve culinary delights but I am tired of having baked chicken for dinner. That reminds me, I have to make a list of cooking pastes to buy before I head back to the la-la-land. Let me know if there's anything I should get for you. I am considering getting you some kurtas from Kolkata. It's going to be different from the chikankari ones you wear, you'll see :). But I think you will like it. After all, I am an encyclopedia on desi hipster fashion and you come tantalizingly close to the bearded, kurta-clad Bangali hipsters I've known. Fun fact: I was always told I'm too Anglicized to be an indigenous hipster :P Now in Amreeka I am merely buying my way into hipster culture—writing at independent coffee shops, swearing by fair trade, partying in warehouses, consuming farm-to-table produce. The upside is that I get to support independent businesses; the downside is I wouldn't be able to do so if I did not have the dollars because being hipster is expensive these days. Unless you remember your days as a grad student in Boston, you will not quite get what I mean. You get paid twice as much being a resident fellow poet or whatever it is they call you. I belong to the cheap labor of an American tier 1 university. The only time I feel well off in the entire year is when I come *home* to Kolkata. Dollars can be put to some good use while I get food and board at *home*. Anyhow, I don't know why I started this rant now.

Well, I haven't accomplished anything other than sleep so far and don't have interesting stories to tell. I did floor mom and dad with some Zaidi-style kesar chai. Mom was like, you never even drank tea while you were here and now look at you lol. At this hour in the evening, when small bells and conch shells from the neighborhood houses elicit gods' blessings, I crave churmur. There used to be a churmur vendor along the tram line past the idol-makers' quarters, which are right by our house. I looked for him on the way back from the airport but couldn't spot his cart. Maybe it was too early in the day, so he wasn't around. I hope he hasn't closed shop, 'cos that will make the trek *home* so much less worth it. Already I feel deeply saddened to be coming *home* at a time when there aren't any festivals to look forward to and the idol-makers' workshops look idle and desolate. All I see are curtains of green and blue tarpaulin with streaks of dried clay on them recalling the frenzy of the autumnal months. I am not a fan of frenzy per se—I just shut the windows to keep at bay the music pouring in from a roadside loudspeaker installed by the local club across our house whose idea of celebration is to play tacky Bollywood or Tollywood music at the loudest possible volume (right now, the Bangla song says "however much you call me foolish and innocent, tomorrow you'll be my bottle of soda!") but there's something about the frenzy of idol-making that draws me. That explains why I do what I do.

I start interviewing the idol-makers in a couple of weeks, that is after I sort out issues with my equipment and have my fill of family gossip over greasy meals with random relatives. Meanwhile, I will have the (dis)pleasure of meeting Rizwan tomorrow. No idea if he's already told you but he comes to Kolkata every now and then, on his way to Bangladesh. Otherwise, as far as I know, he is still based in Delhi. Our common friends from college, Ashwin and Sneha, are getting married tomorrow. Riz is invited and said he'll come. I am so not looking forward to seeing him at a wedding. Weddings bring out the worst in everyone and this is Riz we are talking of...sigh! Don't mind, Zaidi, but I have a legit question (and I know it's kind of inappropriate to ask but when has something inappropriate stopped me lol)—how did you manage to fall in love with Riz? I can scarcely picture anyone drooling over him and least of all, you. He is so opinionated and aggressive. I can imagine people arguing with him but fucking him—No! I bet he was promising the world some revolution the day you met him and in retrospect, I am sure, you know that the revolution did not take off after all. God, this guy was my best bud once. In this very room I remember sitting across the table from him, working away on scripts of plays for hours. Ashwin and Sneha would join in as well but in hindsight, those days seem to be ultimately about Riz and me. When we were in the final year of college, there used to be a protest march in Kolkata every single day for almost a month over the Bengal government's decision to shelter the poet Fatima Ali. She had won an international literary award for her debut collection, which sparked off debates and conflicts. And Riz, during this phase, was obsessed with her Urdu narrative poems. I'm sure you know her work better than I do 'cos Riz used to tell me that she's the rising star of Urdu literature. In fact, if I'm not confusing her with someone else, she perhaps also lived in your hometown for a while after she had to flee Kolkata. After that though I don't know what became of her. Is she a big deal in Urdu literature now? Her long poems were very internal (for the lack of a better word). And it was a pain you-know-where to make plays out of them but Riz wouldn't give up. He was so keen on inventing the wheel rather than riding with what was already there. I guess I liked it at the time. I liked him. Who knows what was up with me those days!

Okay, this club needs to take it easy. I'll go ask dad to talk to them about lowering the volume of their loudspeaker. I am getting a headache. Talk soon.

Ira

7:30 PM

from: Fasahat Zaidi <zaidi.fasahat@h-mail.com>
to: ira.chatterjee12@h-mail.com

Ira,
I hope you're not planning to play your turn-my turn over e-mails throughout the month you are *home*. 72 hours is not enough time for anything new to be up. Since the last time you came in to my apartment, guzzled Jack and Coke, and clogged the drains of our sink, not much has changed.

Not so warmly,
FZ

7:35 PM

from: ira.chatterjee12@h-mail.com
to: Fasahat Zaidi <zaidi.fasahat@h-mail.com>

Oh god, Z, stop acting all hurt. Haven't I apologized profusely? And when you were young like me I'm sure you regurgitated your share of Old Monks and Kingfishers. I will not drink any more when there's a party at your place, okay? Now stop reminding me how grossed out you were when I was gagging. Or don't write while I'm *home*. And for all you know, I might be allergic to cats. I told Mike and you to keep Eliot away from me but you didn't listen.

11: 30 PM

from: Fasahat Zaidi <zaidi.fasahat@h-mail.com>
to: ira.chatterjee12@h-mail.com

Ira, there were no cats at Bodega and yet, we had to swoop you from their floor. You might open beer bottles with bare hands, but you're lightweight. At any rate after your departure, my beard took the right turns and that isn't an altogether negligible development given that I had to facilitate a poetry writing workshop earlier this morning. It was part of the 3-day series for students of color from local high schools, organized by the Diversity and Inclusion Center. While reading your mail, apart from preparing quinoa salad, I was also cooking up prompts to keep the kids engaged for 3 hours. In the end, I simply asked them to imagine losing their childhood *home* and bind the ensuing impressions in a sonnet. The discussions went well, though the students were much less acquainted with the basics like the iambic pentameter than I would've expected. I forget what we learned about form and meter when we were in high school in India. Those were the days when it was alright to begin answers with the insufferable "Shakespeare is a great poet" or go a few words further with "Shakespeare is the greatest poet of all times." On every occasion when a new acquaintance asks if I study Shakespeare after hearing of my literature degree, the ghosts of those answers come to haunt me. I surprise them with my elevator speech about writing ghazals in English. There is something to relish about the face of an interlocutor losing its self-assurance. Today I considered introducing the students to ghazals and rekhti but I held back. I could share a few examples but could they grasp the poems' texture that swiftly? Without understanding the norms of the classical ghazal, it would be impossible to appreciate the subversive playfulness of rekhti. Plus, I would need to check with the Center before discussing explicit sexual content with high school kids.

A messy draft of *Dastaan*'s transcreation is ready. I've got the voice but the words will not sit together just yet. Many more hours of fretting before the words stop wriggling around on the screen and in my head. But on winter afternoons such as these I get engrossed in tracking shafts of sunlight that erase themselves with progressive haste. It is mundane and yet, you don't quite notice until it is too late and the night has fallen, unless you sit next to a glass window remarking the passage of time. Every afternoon I try to absorb the nuances of the spectacle but work interrupts.

Café Rustoroma's masala rooibos chai gets the fraction of cardamoms right up to the thousandths of a milligram, you should try it when you're back. I came here to skim over the assignments that the kids turned in. In a bit I will have to go pick up a second hand microwave. Eliot chewed the cord of the previous one and it stopped working. Instead of splurging on yet another new appliance, I managed to convince Mike to go with craigslist. You were definitely an inspiration on that front, what with your incessant craigslist adventures.

If you happen to see Riz tomorrow, say hi from me. I haven't spoken to him in weeks. As a matter of fact, his and your worldviews are not as antagonistic as both of you make it out to be. Riz would be quite proud of your pithy labor-in-American-University-rant. You know, when I think of him, it's not the words that come back to me. It's the image of him raising slogans in the maddening Delhi heat that sticks out. It was not long after some common friends introduced us. There were these gatherings in which we dined and drank but I hadn't found him particularly attractive then. Riz's intoxicated banter is neither funny nor dramatic. He looks like he is sulking, though really he is not. He becomes a better listener when he is high, he told me. That afternoon, in Delhi, he was gathering students to boycott classes, protesting a faculty's derisive comment in response to a student's written request for equipping the campus with gender neutral toilets. The dean did set up a team to probe the professor's behavior eventually, though Riz was under probation for having incited students to act as he did. The details escape me but I am loath to write off what he did, even though I can't say I agreed with his method.

Ira, you know, your e-mail made me envious of the sound-scape welcoming you *home*. Don't you crave noise while you are here? I crave the sound of trucks from the highways, the cars honking on the roads, people's voices, whirring of ceiling fans. I used to lie on the bed of my hostel in Delhi and run scenarios in my head, conjecturing the destination of those honking vehicles. I would wonder whether any of them were going toward my *home*. What are ammi and abbu doing? This is probably my expatriate nostalgia speaking but due to it I might actually return some day. For good. If you want to do your ethnographic surveys in India, publish them in American peer-reviewed journals, and teach at an American university, our futures might pan out in different continents. One is the world of noise and the other of the noiseless, but both are awash with life.

Cheers,
FZ

1:00 AM

from: ira.chatterjee12@h-mail.com
to: Fasahat Zaidi <zaidi.fasahat@h-mail.com>

Sonnet?? Really, Zaidi? Maybe I am past the point of being charmed by poems that express the male poet's love for the idolized female figure but I find such glorification of unrequited love to be fraught with greater danger (I believe that's the kind of stuff which encourages stalkers. For real.) than a healthy dose of sexual banter. To these kids your adoption of the playful female persona in writing would have been a revelation. Just sayin'. But you're the dude with a nose ring, who pulls off sarees <3. So, I guess you know better.

Btw...can you send me a copy of your version of *Dastaan* when it's done? I told mom about your work. She's acquainted with Urdu poetry owing to her stint in your hometown. She can't read the nastaliq script but she follows the spoken language. So she's curious as to how you write ghazals and rekhti in English. You know, when I was younger I used to hate ghazals 'cos they all sounded the same to me. I even recorded my own voice, reciting "kumor parar gorur gari" and other such poems, over mom's cassette collections :P. She was flabbergasted when, in front of her music students, the tape recorder unleashed white noise and my blabber over the Best of Iqbal Bano. I must have been smacked afterward, though my memory draws a blank now. Anyways, I shall try to sleep now or the jetlag won't go away anytime soon. I can still hear the song on loudspeaker though. Wonder how everyone at *home* snores with that racket in the background.

Ira

Monday, 24 December 2012
11:00 AM

from: Rizwan Syed <s.rizwan85@h-mail.com>
to: ira.chatterjee12@h-mail.com

If u're looking for a camcorder n haven't bought 1 yet, u should ask Sneha. She once lent me her flip camera and voice recorder. At the very least, it'll be better than a mobile phone and in case u're going to ask her, do that soon as she's leaving for her honeymoon day after. Also, just spoke to Fasahat. He told me u're the treasurer for his Urdu club over there. What! I'm sure u can't read a word of the language n I know from experience that people should exercise caution before letting u take up the cause of that 1 language for sure. Best wishes for ur Kumartuli project. It's ur *home* ground, don't screw that up.

During my first visit to Kumartuli, it was so easy to locate ur three story mansion. Ur *home* stood out in a not so desirable way. Does it continue to offer a view of the neighborhood workshops or have real estate agents raised apartments around it already? Remember how we used to go up to the terrace to stealthily smoke and watch the artisans work in the alleys? And the stench of the public urinal from across the block and blobs of crow shit on the terrace, haha. And that bloke you fancied, Ashwin, almost got a row of drying clothes on fire while attempting to light a matchstick. He was so so silly! So were we. He seemed sorted in his wedding regalia. U on the other hand looked and talked just the same. It was good seeing u after so long.

2:00 PM

from: ira.chatterjee12@h-mail.com
to: Rizwan Syed s.rizwan85@h-mail.com

How do you do this, Riz? Your two paragraph e-mail agitates me for two hours. When will you let go of that little incident about Fatima Ali and not make it a part of every communication we EVER have? And you dare not breathe a word about it to Zaidi. Not that it's a big deal but I am really fed up of discussing such a trivial issue with people (read: YOU) for years. I maintain that you wanted us to be heroes (or villains) and this blaming business helps sustain the illusion that we could've been exceptional; we could've been exemplary. So, I am not the only one who talks and looks the same. You resist the very idea of moving on in life.

Even in your best wishes there is a pinch of your trademark snarkiness when it comes to anything having to do with me. But you know what? I know what I am doing here. I have lived in Kumartuli pretty much all my life before moving to the US. There's a reason I decided to dedicate years of my life to researching the art and the people behind that art. My house does not stand out in the ugly fashion you claim it does. Yes, I was not born into a family of idol makers but that does not delegitimize my interest in their work and life. I know and care for them. Some of their children even come to mom's music classes and on more than one occasion mom has offered pro-bono services to them. So yeah, don't come to conclusions based on the little you know.

I will interview as many artists as I can before I even come up with an argument for my PhD thesis. I do have some ideas—for instance, I am interested in the generational aspect of the craft. I am especially interested to find out where women figure in it. How often they inherit the business and how the idol-makers' gender inform their aesthetics. I could sit at *home* and make up my mind about all of this and go find people who affirm what I have to say. However, I don't do that. I am open to the uncertainty this project brings and will let it evolve on its own.

This brings me back to the question of Zaidi's Urdu club. I do not know where that will go. He needed an executive board to get it started and request funds from the university. I volunteered. We plan to promote Urdu music and literature as well as invite authors for readings and so on. Zaidi believes that more people need to understand and appreciate the nuances of his vernacular. And I believe in his vision, and I don't need to read a word of Urdu to do so. You'll be even more astonished to know that the other members of this club include our common friends such as Amber, Xian, Mike et al. They didn't get a word of Urdu either initially but Xian was so stimulated after Zaidi recited poems, explained, and translated them during our monthly meetings that she's opting to learn the language. She will take up a one-year fellowship to do the same which might even slow down her own thesis (She's a poet, you see, who amps up phonetic rhythms through her compositions). Anyways, Riz, I don't intend to prove anything to you with any of this and if you don't trust and respect my ideas, you need not go about looking for cameras for me. I know I had asked you to at Sneha-Ashwin's wedding but I manage fine on my own (the only other people who don't want to believe that I do fine on my own are my parents, for completely different reasons though!). I don't go about poking my nose in affairs of yours with which I think I can't help—do I ever ask you if you've gone *home*?

Ira

Psst: Btw…that urinal was not always there. When I was really young, there used to be a workshop in its place. And, there are no apartment complexes around my house yet but realtors have contacted my family more than once, expressing their interest in turning our house into a flat.

2: 45 PM

from: ira.chattterjee12@h-mail.com
to: Amber Perez <amberscrawls@h-mail.com>

Amby,
Hope all's well with Clara and you. I need to vent. You have heard of Rizwan, right? Well, he is the friend from India that Zaidi and I have in common. I saw Riz at a wedding a few weeks back, after years, because after graduating from college he moved out of Kolkata and would rarely visit. He had a

fallout with his parents and so avoided the city altogether. He did his Masters in Delhi, where he met Zaidi through an NGO. Anyhow, I have been in touch with Riz on and off over e-mails and phone calls through all these years. I sort of always knew what he was up to and vice-versa. I guess because I was so used to playing the bright and shiny Meredith to his dark and twisty Kristina in college that I assumed he should approve of things I did (btw...my Netflix a/c isn't working here, and I am still on season 5 of *Grey's Anatomy*, so no spoilers please). It hurt me when he wasn't all that excited when I decided to go for a PhD. I was almost over that disappointment by this point but he said things at the wedding and over an e-mail that made me doubt myself all over again.

The gist is that he thinks of me as an accomplice to some evil "foreign" force, which plunders local knowledge. He romanticizes the idea of the poor artist and takes me to be an alien correspondent. Many idol makers sell their idols for lakhs of rupees, you know. And here's the thing, if he's referring to the plights of the laborers who work at the workshops, their predicaments are not specific to Kumartuli. It's not like I'll ignore the implicit hierarchies in this trade. For Riz, though, I seem to be the person who becomes part of the problem that they wish to solve—he even uses words like "middle class bourgeoisie" trying to "micro-manage" the less fortunate and so on. I know in my heart that he is wrong but I also worry, what if he is right? What if I am here for all the wrong reasons? Gawd! I don't know. Maybe the easiest solution is not to take this guy seriously at all, which is what I try to do. Nonetheless, whenever I get back in touch with him I get muddled again.

Anyways, I guess I'll forget it soon but right now I needed someone to talk to and mom does not get these things. How's life in California, babe? :) That's the place to be in winter but

every year, something or the other comes up and I don't get
to go. How are you planning to celebrate Christmas? Here
in Kolkata people party all night! Last year when I was in
our desolate la-la-land for Christmas, I was shocked to find
shops and restaurants closed for the day as people spent time
with their families lol. I was expecting galas with free bread
and wine to mark the birth of Christ. Tomorrow evening my
parents are hosting a family get together at *home*. So, I will
miss out on wild parties this year too. Talking of California
though, Riz (okay, I am obsessed with everything he said)
mentioned that Zaidi lived there for years before he came
to the Midwest. Didn't Zaidi do his MFA in Boston? Riz
held that must have been after California but when I told
him that the years don't add up, quite uncharacteristically, Riz
conceded to be mistaken. What's more, in particular, Riz said
Zaidi used to be in San Francisco! Zaidi's going to SFO for
the first time this winter break. So, I am not sure what Riz is
implying. I wonder if he really got things mixed up. It was so
weird (amid all the other kinds of weirdness). Perhaps I am
overthinking. Let me get some work done instead. I still have
to print out all the consent forms for the interviews. After I
left, mom-dad didn't have much use for the printer and it's in
bad shape. Got to get it up and running. Merry Christmas!

Tuesday, 25 December 2012
5:00 PM

From: Rizwan Syed s.rizwan85@h-mail.com
to: ira.chatterjee12@h-mail.com

Dear Ira,
I'm waiting at the Howrah station for my train to Delhi,

which is running 4 hours behind schedule, n pondering how to make the best use of time. Hundreds of people sleep on the platform every day, call this station their *home* but I don't know what to do with my few hours here. The place is more crowded than I would've hoped to be the case on Christmas. Getting to the point, I don't know if 'tis the repetitiveness of this journey from Kolkata to Delhi or the very very short attacks of homesickness I have each time I leave this city, I feel like we've gone through this drill many times—1 of us appears to bowl a bouncer, the other ducks but the delivery hits where it shouldn't, despite the helmet, and then, game over for a while.

We lose touch until an unexpected event flings us back together. Possibly 'tis me who has to let bygones be bygones. Seven years is a long time for holding grudges. I see why Fasahat n u get along. Both of u have the ability to brush aside things n march forward supported by an insatiable yearning for the future. This summer when Fasahat visited, he joined me for some meetings of KARM. We worked together there before he left for the US. He would write slogans for our demonstrations and awareness campaigns as well as chant couplets to gather people for the public lectures and the tamashas <that's what we call our street plays>. He made himself indispensable to the work we were doing but then he transitioned. At the meetings this year it seemed as though he had never left but then again, when he and I travelled to Ajmer Sharif for a couple of days, Fasahat argued against the efficacy of KARM. He tried to persuade me that only a supreme mystical force will set us free from sectarian politics one day. He put it much more eloquently than me, of course, and recited a few couplets to make his point. The naiveté of the assertion is inexplicable, especially when Fasahat is its source. Fasahat n u unnerve me because u both deal with catastrophes the way u would handle the breaking of a vase received as an unwanted gift. U clean up the shit and dispose of the broken parts. But it'll be a long time before we see each other again. Whenever that happens, I hope we'll be friends.

11:45 PM

from: Amber Perez <amberscrawls@h-mail.com>
to: ira.chattterjee12@h-mail.com

Babe,

Greetings from Anaheim. It's an almost-sunny Christmas morning here. These past few days I've been Youtubing 3-D models of the pelvis non-stop. My back is sore from slouching over the phone's screen. I thought I drew hundreds of them in my sleep and in the morning the cacophony of voices offering helpful advice on mastering the pubic symphysis was strong enough in my head to drown the clamor in the kitchen. More caffeine shots, please. I'm supposed to roll tamales for grandma, tio, and tia, visiting from Mexico.

At the moment I am only good for perfecting the elliptical peak that marks out the neutral position of the pelvis... yadadamean. The deadline for turning in the textbook illustrations is around the corner. The pelvis is a star, getting its own page, and next up is the female abdomen presenting the renal artery, calyces, renal pelvis; then, the chest and upper abs with trachea, lungs, bronchial tubes. Everything in charcoal.

My goal is to draw the human anatomy with eyes closed, an exhilarating experience unto itself, though how I wish these gigs paid more. If it did, I would not have to take up the odd part time jobs and spend an arm and a leg on Clara's day care. After this project, I will break up with the imaginary, generic human bodies. The folks who hired me were praising Frank Netter's lifelike sketches of the anatomy but wouldn't shell out a penny to hire models. Can you believe it?! Know what, Netter's drawings were sponsored by drug companies. Need to break into that market but I haven't even looked into how much of it remains, what with the changes in drawing tools and platforms. Heard of Eduard Pernkopf? There's a documentary about his creepy practices on Netflix. The second book in his *Atlas of Topographical and Applied Human Anatomy* presents pictures of the pelvis and the abdomen— great sketches but they're supposedly based on the political prisoners executed by the Nazis. You got to admire and cringe at the same time.

In other news: the med science department from school e-mailed me informing that I can study and sketch the cadavers they own. They have high security rooms populated by dissected corpses on the campus for the med students. I'll get an ID card to access the space, after I fill out a zillion forms :-). Know what, I'd been meaning to do self-portraits. If I have to place organs inside a body, I'd rather it be my body. The anatomical self-portraits could be the focus of my MFA thesis. Now that I get to sketch organs from cadavers, I can juxtapose those or fill those in real human bodies—like my body or your body. Bodies of real people. Volunteer as mah model, gurl. I can't pay you but we'll have rad sessions. And, babe, forget about fellas who make you feel shitty. This Rizwan comes off as a self-important jerk. You needn't reflect on his take on what you are doing. He might be BS-ing about Zaidi to mess with you. I'm sure he knows the kind of influence he and Zaidi have on you. Ignore him. Savor your time at *home*. This is your first visit in two years or no? Have a helluva start to your project, tia Ira, says Clara :-)

Much love,
Amber.

Thursday, 27 December 2012
4:53 AM

from: Fasahat Zaidi <zaidi.fasahat@h-mail.com>
to: ira.chatterjee12@h-mail.com

Ira, Market Street is wreathing yet another effulgent evening. I look out the terrace of this cozy Motor Lodge, merely a couple of blocks from the Castro. Myriad things to see and do but here I am, lapping up the mundane. How did I reach here now? Another day I will be a 17 year old, escorted to the gates of the college hostel by Abbu, following a long journey from *home*. I will be speaking to Ammi over the phone, assuring her I will have food on time and not give in to smoking or drinking. Ammi shall ask Abbu to buy me a soft latex mattress. The most important prop I need to survive college is a good mattress.

I spent most of my day at the Fisherman's Wharf amid a thousand squawking seagulls and slothful sea lions. Did you know sea lions have wings? A bus full of tourists blasted "If you're going to San Francisco," stunning a couple of acrobats contorting to A cappella on the street, entertaining a queue of eager holiday visitors, waiting for the next cruise. Xian guided me through Chinatown; you see, I owed browsing City Lights to that young person who would pace up and down a tiny hostel room reciting "Howl;" its rhythm consuming his breath. But today the image riveted to my mind is that of the concrete, open-mouthed, fire hose along the downtown skyline. Xian recalls Lily, the girl who burst out of her corset and ran amok to contain fire down the Telegraph hill. Over camisole and knickers, she wears double-breasted vests, carries a white silk handkerchief and gambles the night away from under her homburg, unless there's a fire, somewhere, that needs attending. It is the Chinese laundry that is burning. Lily has to get there. Revitalized by the mild earthquake, a storey high wave lashes on Angel Island. One of the detainees there is the laundry owner's son but he has no documents, no language to appease his interrogators, only obscure phonemes and blood.

And stories are always in the present. I find myself rolling on the floor, asleep but not quite. Rewind. Summer in Delhi. Riz is hovering over my head. He wants to go to Ajmer. Meenal gets up and approves of his idea. With my half-open eyes I believe that the idea will fizz out in a few seconds. But of course, it doesn't. Soon we are in a bus speeding through NH8. For the first hour and a half, I practically sleep on the bus. My eyes are itching in the bright sunlight making its way through the glass window. The Aravallis stretching along the wide road is a welcome sight, but I am not yet ready to take in everything with eyes wide open. Meenal is snoring. Riz is up and running though, literally. He gives up his seat to a woman carrying a basket full of hens. The hens are creating a ruckus, inches from my feet. I am partially convinced that I should also give up my seat to other standing passengers. But, the knowledge that we are 3–4 hours away from Ajmer thwarts my largess.

We reach Ajmer in one piece but it is past noon and the Dargah Sharif is closed for an hour. This is not my first visit and like every other time, I sniff the sinister and the serene. Allah restored a blind beggar's sight right outside these gates four centuries ago. Meenal is not carrying anything with which she can cover her head. I lend her my handkerchief. The marble floor of the courtyard surrounding the shrine, peppered with grains for pigeons and pigeon shit, is burning our feet. Once the Dargah re-opens, Meenal and I successfully bow before Khwajaji's shrine. We draw near the divine harmony that is Allah with our eyes closed; the sole barrier to overcome is in our hearts. Nothing else estranges you from me. I am grateful for the snatches of qawwali that replenish me for the days to come. Riz, naturally, does not pray. There is not much else to do that afternoon. We check in to a nearby lodge. The walls of our room have these huge mirrors framed with suitably exotic golden embellishments. The decor does not look bad at all but I keep thinking of your favorite word, 'tacky.' In the evening we go to the Dargah once again. All night, I hear serenades. I know most of these songs from my heart.

The moon is hanging tantalizingly low over the Anasagar Lake, which had once collected itself within a small bowl, offering itself up to Khwajaji. I cast my net far and wide, just in case the moon drops off the sky. But it never does, like the single word repeated at the end of couplets, proximate to the line underneath but not quite there. I try scribbling a few phrases in Urdu after a long time but fail to find a suitable word to rhyme with *inhiraf.* I tell myself, when I manage to mold these into couplets and translate them, I shall write to Ira.

That night in Ajmer was not unlike the nights Rizwan, Meenal, and I spent after listening to the qawwals at the Nizamuddin Dargah in Delhi. Music over food and arguments. Except, this summer, finally Rizwan and I make it *home.* The twinkie I met once comes to who I've become.

Then, he swerves. My jodhpur doesn't budge an inch, though under the skin I am breaking. I give in to his handballing. Some time that night when we're counting blades of the ceiling fan, Rizwan shows me a very old and grainy photo of yours. You have gigantic ear rings on. Ira, we need to be together, soon.

Time to go cruising the Castro.

Warmly,
FZ

P.S: Share the interviews you record. I am always looking for stories.

3

Interviewer: Ira Chatterjee
Location: Kumartuli, Kolkata
Transcriber and Translator: Ira Chatterjee

The interviewees were debriefed about the project and handed a set of prompts on the spot. S/he then spoke freely without the interviewer intervening apart from reassuring remarks or monosyllabic responses such as 'yes', 'certainly,' 'right.' Unless otherwise indicated, the interviewees narrated in Bengali. (-) marks incomplete sentences. [unclear] denotes speech that could not be deciphered.

Wednesday, 26 December 2012
Interviewee #1: Santanu Pal

I have spent approximately 40 years of my life making idols and I was brought up in these lanes. But 3–4 generations back our family was in Rishra. They did not make (-). Kumartuli used to be a place for other kinds of pottery [*chaaker kaj*]; the earlier generations of potters made flowerpot crackers, crockery, vases. Men came with idols on boats from Nadia and Krishnanagar and sold those to rich families—the landholding *zamindars*—on the banks of the Hooghly. Then, some idol makers started to come over annually, right in time for Durga Puja, and they lived with the landholding families for a few months, crafting idols in their houses. My forefathers molded pitchers and made flying flowerpots—those crackers which when lit rocket into the sky—but then the government banned those. At that time, we were leaders in the business and sold flowerpots across India. You see, there were very few potters' houses that could make those crackers. So we were easily at the forefront of the business. When those were banned, we needed a replacement. We have to eat, right? Not every family of potters who lived in Kumartuli those days continue to live here. Many, especially those that specialized in making crackers, left. Idol making gradually became the primary and the only vocation of those who remained. If we get orders then we not only make clay idols, we also [unclear] idols. Krishnanagar is famous for small idols. We specialize in larger ones. Krishnanagar's style is different. We bring the divine face, their models look like dolls. We avoid realism. Idols should not look like real men and women.

All the laborers are 100% Bengali from Shantipur, Medinipur, and other nearby districts. The labor problem is huge here. We have to pay them a daily allowance, give food, and board. This is a big problem. Obviously we can not hire labor abruptly before pujas. They have to be trained for months. These days the government pays Rs. 100 as unemployment allowance in villages (-) lots of rural boys don't come here anymore. If they get Rs. 100 sitting at home, why will they come to earn the same wage through hard work? Here, an unskilled laborer makes only Rs. 100–50 per day. But when laborers become skilled, they even get Rs. 1000 a day. Only

in the puja season. Of course, the [unclear] materials that
cost and then the laborers (-). It is not easy for us to develop
[unclear]. Our next generation wants other work. Should a
farmer's son always remain a farmer?

Talented young boys leave because there's no money in
this trade. My nephew has graduated from the art college.
He has a modern sensibility. He knows of South Indian
and Assamese sculptures. His sensibility helps with theme
pujas. [unclear] us about what they need. Earlier there were
few pujas. Fixed number (-). When people came from East
Bengal, the population increased. 10–15 houses in Salt Lake
flat complexes now have their own pujas. More circulation of
money but raw materials have also become more expensive.
Then, earlier we used drapes and jewellery of clay but now
we are asked to use specific kinds of clothes, jewellery, and
decorations. Overall the idol becomes more expensive.

If people come to see our work from the outside then
it helps us. There was this exhibition. At my workshop, we
sculpted a Muslim fruitseller giving fruits to a Hindu—
Hindu-Muslim brother theme. Where is that sculpture
now? Lying broken, somewhere. Ours is a seasonal business.
Idols exist temporarily. How will our kitchen run if idols
are not immersed and destroyed each year? We get foreign
orders through agents like every other business. We do all
the foundational work, send it out, and [unclear] complete it.
Last September, though, we sent an incomplete idol abroad.
I will show you its photo some time. Those young boys you
see there are decorating an idol for a foreign order. (-) going
to London or California. You have to ask Chand *da*—it's his
order. [unclear] do decorations for weddings nowadays.

The people who come to Kumartuli are interested to see
the process: how we complete such beautiful god's work

despite the conditions in which we live? There have been plans to rehabilitate us. We, of course, would like those to be implemented. But the new transformed locality needs to have lots of open space. Our workshops look dilapidated but they, at least, let the clay models dry. No matter what, we need to place the idols on the street. [It] needs the sun's rays. Clay idols need air and sun. If they uproot us from here and put us in concrete rooms, it will just not be enough. If the sun's rays and air don't circulate, then the straw will start to rot in the dampness. The idol remains in our workshop for months. We deliver it to our clients in the Ashwin month. The kind of space we artisans require is very specific. If they give me a room to work and then raise three-four floors and other kinds of people enter the building, then it will be a problem. Development also means that they will broaden the streets, lorries will enter…we will not be able to keep the idols on the street.

Working with huge clay models requires physical strength. That's why you will not find many women in the workshops. How will women do all this? I know of one Kakon Pal who runs a business. She took over her husband's and father's businesses after her husband died. She is not a real artist. I don't have daughters but if I did I would not encourage them to join this trade. I did not even encourage my son to join this trade. He studies computers and will get to work in office. News people often come to record the process of idol making. They want to see everything, step by step. How we worship the bamboo frame [*kathamo puja*], bind the straw, knead the clay, put it on the straw frame. You should go to see the idols in Chand Pal's workshop. Click its photo. You can talk to them. It will be very useful for your work.

Friday, 28 December 2012
Interviewee #2: Shyamal Mukherjee

Always remember that the *babu* pujas became community puja because of the idol-makers of Kumartuli. If not for them, Ma Durga could not be brought down to the streets for the festivities. That is the number one thing to keep in mind. Kumartuli has contributed to the mood of Kolkata. Kolkata is known for joy. You know that, right? You understand English, right?* It is better if I can speak in English. My tourist friends can also understand.

Calcutta is famous because we know how to smile. Every city is a city for existence but we know how to keep the smile (-), that is Calcutta. Smile means merriment, merriment means festivity, festivity means the worship of statues. So, festival means them—the idol makers. They are part and parcel of Calcutta life. Number two, they know... how they know, you should research that. We have 330 million gods and goddesses. How they look (-). Which book they follow? They don't follow a book. But they know it from memory. How they know that a Demon should be green in color? But Rama is also green in color!† Which color indicates it is good or bad? You should research that. I am showing tourists around these lanes for decades. I know all these artists. But I don't know what they know. And women artists? No, there are no great women artists here. I know of one from the 70s or 80s. But the girl did not last in the idol-making business. There are great artists here. Men, but they are better than many artists in the world.

* The interviewee speaks in English from this section to the end of his narration.

† Rama is blue, though.

Friday, 28 December 2012
Interviewee #3: Abinash Paul

You see Kumartuli is a university today. Whole world [unclear]. From Kumartuli, models and idols go to London, Paris, America. The relatives of those abroad come here to contact and commission us. It is a word of mouth network for the most part. Suppose you see our idol and like it at a puja. When your relative from abroad wants an idol, you recommend us. Then there are also middle men who handle everything. Nowadays because of websites we get orders directly sometimes. We had an exhibition in Kumartuli years back but in general we don't have suitable atmosphere for exhibition. The quality of work needs to be altered before we have good exhibitions. Tourists come to see Kumartuli. They show us in Hindi films whenever they show Kolkata.

Many changes have come about over the years. Earlier there were merely a few houses making clay idols. Now artists use fiberglass, stone, bronze. Currently, there are at least a dozen boys working here who have graduated from the art college. What is more, these are boys who came first in the whole section of the college. Idol-making is a distinct subject though. There are always other kinds of artwork: interior decorations, decorating wedding venues is a new thing. Sculpting often [unclear]. The idol-making business is seasonal. That continues.

But there are also lots of differences between artists growing up here and those who train in art colleges. In art colleges you learn about the whole world. You need to know art history. Modern art and sculpture have different theories. In addition, style is different for eastern and western art. We start with straw, they start with iron. The formally trained artists have different work culture. But after so many boys who graduated from art colleges came here, their company inspired the other boys to learn. Now they are doing good work. You know, sometimes other renowned artists in the city lure trained laborers from here, they use their training, which we provide. Anyhow, the learning system of art college has influenced us. See, I graduated from art college in '65. My sons and nephews have graduated from there, majoring in painting and sculpture. They are trying to improve the work by making it realistic.

For making idols also you need realism. Suppose a Durga idol. In the Rajbari pujas, devi Durga's ride, the lion, would look like horses. The eyes of the goddess would have large and elongated lashes. Any onlooker would know it to be stone eyes, not real eyes. Now the demon, Mahishasur, looks like a real human being. The buffalo looks like a real buffalo, the snake looks like a real snake. This difference has come about. Now more clothes and jewelry (-). A new trend has started in the Kolkata pujas. Different prizes are offered for the idols that are ranked first, second, and third. This has provided impetus for improving idols. See how the straw is being bound here: that also has a theory. Idol-making is commercial work. Then there are commissioned projects. Each family has its own style. For instance, our style is different from the artists who came here from East Bengal. We don't need to write our names on the idols we make; if you are a connoisseur you can make it out from looking at the idol. You can look at the idols that we make in our workshop and know that it is from Ashesh Paul's house. Ashesh Paul is my grandfather's name.

We have been here for seven generations. (-) here from Krishnanagar. Krishnanagar dolls would be sold on the banks of Hooghly. The potters have been here from the time of Job

Charnock. You know about Job Charnock? Kumartuli was created long back. The place where we are sitting now used to be a Hogla forest. Ganges was closer to this side. That dom Kali there, you know which one I am talking about? The doms would pray to that idol because that area was a cremation ground. From that time (-). The business and art flourished closer to the river. Obtaining clay and transporting the finished models was easier because of the river. From that time we have Kumartuli. It is not today. But from the days of Job Charnock.

Three villages together made up Kolkata. Sutanuti, Kalika, Gobindopur. By Sutanuti we mean—there is Hatkhola on this side, no? There used to be a market selling threads—*suta*. The village got its name from that market. That's why (-) Sutanuti. Gobindopur was this other side. And Kalika is the current Kalighat. Three villages. Together they made up Kolkata.

I have three sons. Idol-making is our family business. It is something we have inherited. But making pratimas [idols] is such a feat that no one person can pull it off alone. We need help. There are processes one after another. Right from constructing the bamboo framework. We decorate idols once again in the pandal. In between there was a craze for Durga idols made of coins, grains, and other such materials, to go with the themes of the pujas. Now that fad has subsided. So we are again back to doing good work.

In art colleges there are women who sculpt. Here you won't find many. Some women work with the smaller models, the dolls, or slip-cast idols. But that is about it. I think guide Shyamal was talking of Pranoy Paul's family. There was a girl in their workshop. I don't know the whole story. She played around with sculpting idols for a while. She did something to the face of the Durga pratima and some of the pujas that year noticed it and kept commissioning similar faces. There was a lot of fuss about it that year but it all died down. You won't find them now. They closed down their business after Pranoy Paul's son died.

Wednesday, 2 January 2013
Interviewee #4: Kakon Pal

I do not sculpt idols though my family has been in the idol-making business for five generations. Both my father's and mother's families were into idol-making and then my husband's family was the same way. It was only after my marriage that I moved to Krishnanagar. I grew up here. Idol-making is not something we women think about. Our family's livelihood depends on it and if we think of idol-making, it is [unclear]. I hardly came to my father's workshop and I was not taught how to sculpt. I had no interest in it either. But no one born here can simply not know a thing about idol-making. It is in our blood.

When my husband died, his brother took over the business in Krishnanagar. My brother-in-law is not a bad man but when all the work is done by him, it is natural that his wife and children will benefit. He took care of us too but it was not enough. I would be happy to continue that way if I had no children. But I had two daughters and they were still in school. My husband wanted them to study and so did I. Nowadays studying is important. Even to get them married (-). They should not have to join this trade.

So I decided to join the business and look after my husband's share. I do not have difficulties in overseeing the work. I have kept laborers, that my husband had trained, on my payroll. They came with me to Kumartuli from Krishnanagar. I also managed to recruit some others after coming here. I run my own business but I also get the support from my father's side. Also there is more money in Kolkata than in Krishnanagar. Everyone wants to get their idols from Kumartuli. About a year back, in October 2011, we sent idols to Delhi and Bombay. There are not many women like me in Kumartuli though there are more than 150 families making idols here. My father may still know. You can interview him. He knows more about idols than I do. He is suffering from arthritis. So he does not come to the workshops that often anymore. If you keep visiting the workshops in the afternoon, you may find him one of these days.

4

Search: *Lucknow*
Friday, 4 January 2013
8:15 PM

from: ira.chatterjee12@h-mail.com
to: Fasahat Zaidi <zaidi.fasahat@h-mail.com>

Z, looks like I'll be stuck at Chicago airport for the night :(
The flight was supposed to leave by 6 but these airline walas
told me it will be delayed by a quarter of an hour and then
again by half an hour. Now it's past 8 and they are like, sorry
no more flights tonight. This is why I hate flying through
Chicago. It's always a nightmare. I hope they don't lose my
luggage (I've got four kurtas for you, poet :-)). I asked these
airline people to pay for my hotel, at least, but they couldn't
care less. The lady here tells me that I should sleep at the
airport! Then she'll put me on the first flight to our la-la-
land tomorrow morning. Do you know anyone in Chicago? I
need a couch to crash tonight, and no, I ain't sleeping on the
uncomfortable seats here. Dad's friends live near Hyde Park
but they also went to India over the break and aren't back yet.
Wait…the lady is calling me.

Okay, so looks like they have scheduled one last flight at 10 PM and the lady's put me on the waitlist for that. She's not so bad after all :P. I hope I make it. I am so exhausted with everything. I expected to find more women among the idol makers. It's strange you know—I grew up there and I have been to many of the workshops as a child. My dad went to kindergarten with some of the idol-makers and when he learned about my project, he thought he would contact the artisans he knew and bring them over to our house for the interviews. I stopped him because fieldwork's all about going to the field and not calling people over for interviews! (dad asks, what's the difference?) Anyhow, you know, I saw this project as my way of giving back to the community which, due to its sheer proximity, has been an essential part of who I am. What I found out in the process, however, is that I did not know the people and their work enough. Apparently, there are zero female idol-makers. Mom and Dad had stated as much but I felt that I had seen women working there. Have I made up my memories? I recall women painting the idols lined up in the alley. I am sticking my body through the steel bars of the terrace, 'cos I am tiny in this memory, and peering at the movement of their hands. Riz was surprised when I told him about my interest in women as idol-makers—he knows so little of the place but even he had known that I was headed in the wrong direction! That hurts. But there must have been a few women, some women, at least one woman, to have tried her hand at idol-making. It's impossible that no woman would be interested in something like this. 'Cos if I were born into a family of idol-makers, I would certainly, at least, try to work and find out if I am any good. Maybe it's not as easy but I hope I am not delusional about this.

Btw… I had an interesting co-passenger on the long flight from Delhi to Chicago (thank god!). He's a (rich) consultant at a firm based in this city but he's originally from *Lucknow*. It's funny how I've never been to *Lucknow* but keep bumping into people who have something to do with the city. This person moved out of *Lucknow* about 15 years ago and has been in the US ever since. So he is not up to speed with the goings on there and I asked him about the contemporary music and poetry scene, which mom and you talk of all the time. He said I know as much about all that as you do… lol. This time he had gone to *Lucknow* for his social wedding. He had married one of his colleagues in the US but had aging relatives in India who wanted to eat at a wedding. So he humored them by marrying the same woman twice. The person sitting next to the *Lucknow* man was obnoxious. He was ordering bottle after bottle of Chardonnay (it wasn't complimentary after the first one) and it sure felt like he was joining the Half Mile High club. What bothered me was that he was sweating and stinking. Anyways, now I will go hover around the airline lady, so that she gets me off the waitlist and puts me on the flight just to get rid of me. Tada!

Saturday, 19 January 2013
11:22 PM

from: ira.chatterjee12@h-mail.com
to: Fasahat Zaidi <zaidi.fasahat@h-mail.com>

Z, sorry that I couldn't stay longer at your place this evening. Mike, Xian, and you were fantastic and I would've loved to be around when you guys opened the floor to the audience (and your shorba was out of this world) but I had promised to look after Clara through Amby's graveyard shift tonight. I wonder where she gets the energy to bake and deliver Midnight Cookies for the extra bucks after all the grad school work! Clara is asleep now. So, I guess I did good :-). I was thinking of the magazine you showed us today. I know you said it's published in *Lucknow* by your friend Tausif and it's called *Taqreer*, none of which sounded familiar. However, I have a hunch that I've seen the header of the magazine somewhere else. And that's intriguing given my ignorance when it comes to little Urdu magazines in general. The only logical connection I can make is with the magazines that Riz used to show us. Did *Taqreer* ever publish poems by Fatima Ali? She used to write for several magazines before publishing the collection that resulted in the attacks against her. Actually she continued to publish underground even after fleeing her hometown in Bihar. Riz, because he was possessed by her work at the time, used to collect these magazines. Does *Taqreer* circulate in Kolkata? The last time when I asked whether you knew about Fatima Ali, you said you had merely heard of her. So, maybe I am wrong but you can check with Tausif.

11:45 PM

from: ira.chatterjee12@h-mail.com
to: Rizwan Syed <s.rizwan85@h-mail.com>

Oi Riz, was *Taqreer* (a quarterly publication from *Lucknow*) one of the little magazines you showed me with poems of Fatima Ali?

Friday, 1 February 2013
10:33 AM

from: Lavanya Chatterjee <chatterjeelavanya@h-mail.com>
to: ira.chatterjee12@h-mail.com

dear Ira,
the moment you go back to the other continent, you forget about your mom dad. do you know how many times i and your papa call you on the phone last night? i know you will give the same excuse, your phone was on silent, but what is a phone for if you do not take calls or return calls? i even message you and no reply to that. one day some emergency will happen and you will not know because you will not pick up your phone. i never call you for fun. it is important if i call you 10 times. your shona pishi's brother-in-law passed away yesterday. he used to give you currants and cashews every time you visited shona's house. there was such a line for cremation at neemtala. We had to wait and wait. your shona pishi was so broken. even your mejka called from germany. i phoned you so you could talk to her but no answer from your side!

had i known how long we would be up last night, i would cancel this evening's music class. it was so tiring. these days i find it difficult to stand for hours like that. the kids in my class don't make life any easier. they only want to learn film songs. fevicol se, chikni chameli, kolavari. i say how will you sing anything in tune if you do not know your sa re ga ma pa dha ni sa? but that will not do. they have to start with hindi songs which no playback singers sing. only computers sing those songs. among film songs also the kids don't learn the melodious ones. they say those are for the old people. but do i depend on the fees they pay? if i need the money to run the kitchen then it is another matter. i will have to dance to their tunes. actually people here have no taste. it is not like what it was in *lucknow*. people were so refined and cultivated. what a shock it was to me after i got married and came here! had my parents lived, they would cancel this match with your father based on the looks of the locality. but my uncles only looked at your dad's family and salary. so i landed in this kumartuli. high lineage but no running water from the tap. a well inside the bathroom to store water brought from the municipality taps twice a day. year round dampness.

i read your friend fasahat's poems. they are nice. but because i did not go to english medium the way you did, i don't get the essence from them. i see what he does with the voice, the freeness about sex he brings but i still like ghalib, mir, faiz, and the original ghazals much much more than these sorts of poems. you tell me that fasahat recites his poems at bars wearing saree over jodhpurs, with people staring at him. is that not so gimmicky? he tries to rub things in people's faces. that is the very opposite of the subtlety of the original ghazals. ghazals have long tradition of mixing male-male love with love for the god. old trick. ghazal's mashuqs are often male lovers. also there is that saqi, the wine bearer—another guy. but original ghazal poets did not need to wear sarees to make the point or use foul words. also, he uses so many open couplets. in ghazals each couplet works as a self-contained unit of thought. the open couplets make his poems so much more disordered. don't tell fasahat i said all this. if he asks, tell him i found his poems very good. i don't want your friendship to be ruined because of my preferences. call me old fashioned.

when i was learning from ustad shafiulla khan saab in *lucknow*, if there is one word i learned to associate with ghazals, it is most surely, finesse. he used to say, your voice should be like the soft muslin that passes through a finger ring without getting its threads caught in the metal's intricate design. the lyrics were part of the delicate balance. early on sunday mornings i would take a rickshaw from new hyderabad, which was just about expanding then, to thakurganj where ustadji lived and taught. aah…those misty mornings swinging on the balcony next to which ustadji sat with his eyes closed, sitar in hand, filling the room with his ethereal voice. it was a different era. some days i reached to find ustadji immersed in his riyaz. i would wait. all the other girls would also wait. my students here, on the other hand, can not even wait a few seconds for me to come and open the door. they ring the doorbell five times in one minute. we tiptoed so as not to disturb ustadji. my students start a riot the moment they cross the threshold.

lakhnavi tehzeeb, ira, outshines everything else. what courtesy people had! especially the khandani muslims of *lucknow*. they were so pretty too. you can make out that they descended from the nawabs. new hyderabad was on one side of gomti and the old city, where the more traditional muslim families lived, was on the other side. i saw such khandani people up close because of my friendships. when i was in class five or six, our batch mostly had hindu girls. you know that because the muslim girls always come in burqas. there was one muslim girl, mahek. not many other girls speak to her during the lunch breaks. so, i walk to mahek one day and ask if i can eat her tiffin. she refused saying i shouldn't eat because i am a brahmin. i told her that she can eat my tiffin too but she wouldn't relent. meanwhile, the entire class stared at us! entire class! after lunch break simran argued that muslims cook cows and we should not eat their food. i remember the incident vividly because mahek's refusal was very very strange. when i ask my parents if it is alright for me to take food from muslim girl, they say we should share food with one and all and i can exchange any food item with mahek as long as the item contains no beef. that's because beef has tapeworm and it's the same reason why i ask you to avoid steak. hindus and muslims were there everywhere in *lucknow* and there was no tension. only the shias and sunnis fought among themselves but that was of no concern to us, hindus.

later i become a very good friend of mahek. simran too became friends with her because of me and then we visit mahek's house from time to time... mahek's brothers were indeed very handsome. they gave us scooter rides to parks around their house. they were tall, fair, had high cheekbones, brown eyes, dark black arched eyebrows, long eyelashes. and the way they spoke! full of politeness and courtesy. imagine my shock when i came to this kumartuli where i find people like bhola outside the window and the potters. where was *lucknow* and where is this. i don't recall going to the place fasahat is from—asharfabad, na? but i think it will be like aminabad. old *lucknow* is so congested. the lanes are like a maze. there are so many shops in aminabad. mostly muslim families live there. it is also the place to buy cheap, decent things. hazratganj was the more posh marketplace. obviously the more expensive one too.

why you like this fasahat so much i don't understand. he writes like this and wears saree and nose ring. already i know he is gay, like rizwan. how will you find someone for yourself if you always hang out with gay muslim people? rizwan was your age at least; fasahat is 10 years older you tell me. a different generation almost. you have come a long way from the time you dropped your cousin's baby to babysitting for friends. now don't spoil your chances by spending your

time listening to gay people read poems. to tell you the truth
i don't fully support your babysitting either. you went there
to study, not to look after other people's children. so don't
let such things come in the way of your career. look out for
yourself. over there, your papa and i are not there to do that.
take care and phone us.

Mummy.

12:15 PM

from: ira.chatterjee12@h-mail.com
to: Lavanya Chatterjee <chatterjeelavanya@h-mail.com>

Mom, I slept early yesterday and noticed your missed calls just
now. I am on my way to class. Will come back and respond
in detail. The *Lucknow* anecdotes were sweet :) but I do think
that you are talking of a particular kind of ghazal and culture
and it's not the whole picture. FYI: I like Zaidi because he
is real and I like his poems for their chance connections,
juxtapositions, shifting voices…the run-on lines and the
open couplets: where you reach the end of a verse thinking
you know what is coming but the following part sitting in the
next line tweaks, even reverses the sense. Zaidi can also take
criticism in his stride—so no worries about thy comments,
mater. Anyways, seriously, I got to go now and please! dad
and you shouldn't freak out if I don't take a few calls. And btw,
don't respond to this e-mail saying, you shouldn't tell us not
to worry because you are not a parent.

Saturday, 2 February 2013
2:15 AM

from: Fasahat Zaidi <zaidi.fasahat@h-mail.com>
to: ira.chatterjee12@h-mail.com

Ira, you brought memories of those havelis falling like melting wax of the old quarters wrapped in crumbling plaster, of the homogenization in the name of development. Your mother should go to Gomtinagar today. She will find nothing of her *Lucknow* there. What lie buried beneath today's nondescript apartments alone can sustain her story. Stories can be razed, not stories, yet who heeds their murmur? I am buying tickets to *Lucknow* for summer. My manuscript ought to be finished and submitted before the funding runs out in 2014 and the shade of moist khas khas is my sole hope of any progress in that direction. The scented candles you bought are not helping. They are overpowering my senses and clogging the flow of memories. You have to repay me for choking with these plastic scents by keeping company during my antique shop-hop this weekend. Since you come from a family of hoarders, as you put it, I am always counting on you.

Friday, 22 February 2013
11:45 PM

from: Fasahat Zaidi <zaidi.fasahat@h-mail.com>
to: ira.chatterjee12@h-mail.com

Ira, do you happen to have my copy of *Lucknow: A Forgotten History*? It's not on my bookshelf. No doubt the papers are richer in color for you having read it but I need it back.

Wednesday, 13 March 2013
09:13 PM

from: Amber Perez <amberscrawls@h-mail.com>
to: ira.chattterjee12@h-mail.com

Babe,

I'm officially over the Midwestern winter. Sigh! This weather
is just not for me. No matter how many cups of your masala
chai I gulp, my nose bleeds, eyes water, head feels as though it
were stuck in a refrigerator. The prospect of shopping for rad
peacoats and parkas ain't making the weather any attractive.
Clara's got less of California in her than me and fares much
better. Usually, after battling piles of snow, the classrooms we
find ourselves in are heated. However, this cadaver-sketching
business has landed me in eerily cold rooms that smell of
formaldehyde.

I had the permission to work there for 6 hours at a stretch
today. I was stoked knowing I would make some solid progress
but after a little over 3 hours my fingers and eyes were done. I
came out for breaks, stood in the snow to rejuvenate/re-freeze
myself, but my hands wouldn't do their job. The sight of pale,
wrinkly skin of the cadavers was fucking gnarly. As a senior, I
had a semester-long date with cadavers for an elective and I
wasn't one of those folks who excused themselves and rushed
outta labs. Of late I youtube cadavers too much, which,
methinks, contributes to the weird feeling in my gut. While
drawing the lines, I can not not think of the good and the
bad practices that led to the preservation of the body lying in
front of me. It could have been an unclaimed corpse—no one
interested in burying it; or a donation from a well-wisher;
or a body sold for the profit of two to three grands. The best

cadavers are bodies of the young, taut and in good overall shape. How freaky is that! The woman I was looking at today wasn't all that young. Her body has been on this campus for at least two years. I got to get over such details; they should be of no consequence to me while sketching. Anyway, I returned early. Good for my roomie who was on Clara duty. This also means I got to ask to go back there to complete the sketch again on Friday. Hence, your and my Friday evening session will have to be postponed. Are you free Saturday morning? You could come over. I'll treat you to a pancake breakfast before you pose for me.

Too tired to read for the art history class tomorrow. The class is interesting but I should've enrolled for the section focusing on anatomy offered last autumn. The art enterprise class I'm taking is more useful. The prof there organizes panels with alumna who make money from their artwork. Know what, now that I think of it, you might want to take the course next semester. It's sure to offer perspective on the business angle of the art form you're considering. Idol-making is a business on which an entire community's livelihood depends, isn't it? Economics hand in hand with aesthetics. This class is all about that. I could see how this may be useful for Fasahat as well. He mentions the changing culture of his *Lucknow* and with it the ever depleting support for the arts. As a resident poet is he allowed to take classes? The prof is nice and won't mind if Fasahat wants to sit in for select sessions. I can tell you guys more about the class in case it interests you. Let me know about Saturday.

Amber

Tuesday, 9 April 2013
10:23 PM

From: Rizwan Syed <s.rizwan85@h-mail.com>
to: ira.chatterjee12@h-mail.com

Rizwan: Hey Ira! There?

me: Yes. You don't reply to e-mails in months, Riz!

Rizwan: Sorry, was pinging about that only. ur mail had slipped through the cracks n I have been very busy the last few months, even missed Dhoni's double century in the 1st test against Australia. KARM is collaborating on an outreach programme that requires us to travel to specific villages, live there, set up basic healthcare facilities, and win the trust of the villagers and the panchayat so as to be able to encourage safe sex practices. I am assigned to Sirihara Kund near the Bihar-UP border.

me: Hmm…I see. Wait, isn't that where Fatima Ali was from?

Rizwan: No, her family was from Saleempara in Madhuban, not very far from Sirihara though. Why are you so into Ali's whereabouts?

me: arre…I asked you about *Taqreer* in the mail toh

Rizwan: Fatima Ali had been publishing in newspapers and zines from the early 2000s and *Taqreer* was actually one of the first platforms to publish her. This was long before she won the Gutzwiller Prize for her poetry collection. *Taqreer* continued to publish her work even after the fatwa was issued.

me: And *Taqreer*'s editor-founder is Zaidi's friend Tausif? Then, why does Zaidi say he doesn't know if the magazine published Ali?

Rizwan: Well, Tausif, or Dr Tausif as he is known in *Lucknow* circles, has been publishing *Taqreer* since the late 1980s. He was a homeopathic doctor by day and worked on issues of *Taqreer* by night. Never married. He is too unwell to practise medicine any more but indefatigably puts together issues of the magazine. I am not certain when Fasahat got personally acquainted with Dr Tausif but it might have been after Ali stopped publishing in *Taqreer*, or anywhere really, due to the repeated death threats.

me: So Ali does not write at all anymore?

Rizwan: There hasn't been a single publication under her name in at least five years. Why are u digging up that history? I told u last time, let's leave that behind us.

me: This isn't about your and my fallout over the street play in college. I have left it behind. It is about Fasahat. You know he wrote to me from San Francisco and the e-mail was so touristy. I asked him whether he had ever lived in the city but he denied.

Rizwan: Yes, that makes sense. I told you I got it mixed up with someone else. With the kind of work I do, I meet too many people with long and circuitous travel histories.

me: But Fasahat is different, right? You had a relationship with him.

7 minutes

Fasahat's earliest publications are from around 4 years ago.

Rizwan: Were u googling that?

me: no, I know

Rizwan: What is ur point n what does Fatima Ali have to do with it?

me: I don't know… you guys are not telling me something.

Rizwan: About what?

me: I don't know.

Rizwan: If you don't know, then I can't help. I got to go, Ira. Take care!

Wednesday, 10 April 2013
4:25 AM

from: ira.chatterjee12@h-mail.com
to: Rizwan Syed <s.rizwan85@h-mail.com>

Oi Riz, didn't you visit *Lucknow* for the first time in 2008? We had not talked for about a year at the time but you responded to my ping and said you were with a friend in *Lucknow*. Who was the friend? I found the chat transcript and it says that you were in Asharfabad, where Zaidi is also based. So how was this friend related to Zaidi? See, here's the transcript:

---Forwarded message begins here---

from: Rizwan Rizwan <s.rizwan1212@h-mail.com>
to: ira.chatterjee12@h-mail.com
date: Tue, Apr 15, 2008 at 11:30 AM

me: Rizzzz

Rizwan: u are actually initiating a chat? I thought u had blocked me.

me: wth… Even you can initiate conversations if you like. It took me a while to add this new ID of yours. Why did you change your hocus pocus one?

Rizwan: u changed u to you. Why?

me: I rarely used sms type contradictions bey :P

Rizwan: Yeah, right.

So, what's up?

me: *contractions

Nothing. Simply catching up with ya.

Rizwan: Noble reason to ping, though unfortunately our conversation has to be brief. I am about to have lunch and then go for a meeting.

me: Okay. What meeting?

Rizwan: I am in *Lucknow*, meeting the coordinator of an NGO. They support kothis and MSMs who are HIV+.

me: Official excuse to meet other gay men? ;)

Rizwan: I don't need an excuse for that. This is all work and no play.

me: lol :P btw...I have never met a real HIV+ person.

Just sayin'. Now don't call me insensitive for owning up to facts.

Rizwan: hmph

me: When will you return to Dilli?

Rizwan: In a couple of days. I only have one meeting scheduled here but I am staying in a friend's house in Asharfabad. She has come down with me and wants to spend a few more days here. Why?

me: I might accompany Dad when he goes to Delhi during the holidays.

Rizwan: Let me know the dates, I'll show u around. But have u decided what u want to do after your MA?

me: Dude, there's still a while to go before my MA classes even begin. Anyhow, Sneha and I are considering journalism.

Rizwan: I thought u would want to become a professor.

me: Do you like kothis?

Rizwan: u tell me what kind of men u like. Then we can compare notes.

The guy I am supposed to meet today was jailed for helping prevent the spread of HIV among gay men. He was 'caught red-handed' distributing condoms to kothis in a Hazratgunj Park, in the heart of the city. When the kothis intervened, the police left but they kept tracking him. In a month they caught him again and this time they would not let him go. Carrying condoms was his crime because apparently that abets 'unnatural sex'. The state wants us dead, as if we deserve HIV for daring to live.

me: How long was he in jail?

Rizwan: Three whole months. He was not even granted bail.

me: This business sounds risky ya. What work are you doing with the NGO?

Rizwan: I eventually want to join them full time to mobilize people like us. We need to support one another and stand up for our rights.

If I organize a workshop for human rights awareness in time for this year's pride march in Kolkata, do you think you will be willing to help?

me: 'course ya! Btw, have things improved between you and your parents?

Rizwan: I try not to think about it. On the last occasion I was in Kolkata, I stayed with friends.

me: I can ask my parents. You can stay at our place too if you want.

Rizwan: Thanks but I now have friends within the community who look out for me.

me: So is this *Lucknow* friend also from the community?

Rizwan: Why? :-)

me: 'Cos you only stay with people from your little community.

Rizwan: This friend...u would like her after all

Today she woke up at 7 in the morning to get the freshest makhan malai, set to perfection by the morning dew, from a vendor who does the rounds of these lanes on a bicycle.

me: Ouf <3

Rizwan: Delicious treats but perhaps, a few decades from today, this will be the stuff of legends.

12:17 PM

From: Rizwan Syed <s.rizwan85@h-mail.com>
to: ira.chatterjee12@h-mail.com

Ira, what's ur deal? u r wasting time digging up 6-year-old chat transcripts! Has ur doctoral project come to this? I am jealous of the sheer amount of free time on ur hands. Have u found the female idol-maker u were looking for? Or has that stopped mattering to u? Just so u stop bugging me, the friend in this chat is Meenal. She was also from *Lucknow* and lived in Asharfabad. Also, I am not answering any more e-mails that involve squandering time over nonsense. Use ur detection skills where it counts rather than for spying on friends' private lives.

Monday, 13 May 2013
5:30 PM

from: Fasahat Zaidi <zaidi.fasahat@h-mail.com>
to: ira.chatterjee12@h-mail.com

Ira, in the ruins of one world, another finds its spark. That
is the two-century-old bond tethering Delhi to *Lucknow*.
Journeying from Delhi to *Lucknow* today is like walking
between two parallel mirrors. My language and my story
are trapped in this route, eternally recurring in reverse. Each
instance of recurrence diminishes its scope and compromises
its stature. It is curious how, even before I knew anything
about *Lucknow*'s history in any formal sense, I lived with the
anxiety that this city might flicker out of existence as though it
were a reflection of some other time and place. Your mother's
Lucknow is a stable city. It is stable even in its decadence. My
Lucknow shrinks and expands overnight, contingent on the
slope of light, on the turn of season. This flickering premise, I
kept convincing myself, can solely endure in language, as Urdu.

Abbu and Ammi were disappointed when I relinquished
the path leading up to the august world of medicine. As a
homeopathic doctor, Abbu wanted his elder son to become
bigger and better. That meant a general physician, if not
something even more specialized and sophisticated. This elder
son, on the other hand, was happily preparing to ruin himself
because laws of inheritance suggested that the ruins were his.
Ammi's and Abbu's shocked demeanor when I expressed my
desire to major in Urdu was beyond my reckoning. Studying
Urdu, Abbu said, would be worse than not attending college
at all. Ammi asked if I intended to spend my life reading
stories and writing poetry, why did I not take birth as a girl?

Following days of struggle we struck a deal. If studying a language, reading and writing stories was what I was going to do, then the only acceptable option was English. English would make me employable. Even if as a clerk. But in college, along with English, I kept at Urdu. The Urdu classes had very few students. The experience of learning was intimate, the lessons anecdotal.

Before Ghalib's letters and poems decried the demise of Urdu with the destruction of old Delhi's markets, forts, and lanes, Mir, the ustad who even the pompous Ghalib swore by, had been forced out of that city's courts. Sitting in Urdu classes, I would see Mir enter the streets of *Lucknow* clad in a plain angrakha and qalpaq. Now Mir is a poet-genius, the court ought to revere him for his simplicity. He throws in a richly decorated but worn out katzeb, spun out of cotton with wide silk borders, just because. This is Mir, celebrity poet of the Delhi Durbar, ladies' man. Mir, who would but die for each woman he has loved and there are many. Our poet is not alien to journeys. After all, Shahjahanabad was only his adopted address. But what does he find in *Lucknow*? A crass durbar that is worse than the ruins of Shahjahanabad. His Lakhnavi colleagues at Asaf-ud-Daulah's do not share his vocabulary, taste, or humor. Instead of learning a thing or two from the sire of Urdu poetry, they laugh at him. Feelings of dislike and distrust are mutual. To Mir, the mushairas in *Lucknow's* Chowk are a joke. No sophisticated repartee exchanged among court poets, sipping wine while sitting on ornate diwans. Straight fights. Cocks, kites, and poets fight not only within walled compounds but also on the streets. And there are those audacious low-caste women who discuss cocks of the other kind and giggle in their zubaan. The drawstrings here are loose and if you love, you don't die but laugh. No wonder that Insha, who did not find takers in Delhi, finds patrons here. That ustad of the profane does not know the first thing about the melancholic cravings of mashooq. He fools around, using an effeminate pseudonym, weaving dastaans eulogizing the battle of bangles and the knotty sisters. Thankfully, *Lucknow* turns out to be a great leveler in the end. Both Mir and Insha die poor, bereft of patronage.

Meanwhile, Asaf-ud-Daulah himself spends time with Claude Martin, running elaborate copy-and-paste programs: lift ideas of minarets, gateways, and domes from Delhi and Turkey and plant them in *Lucknow*. *Lucknow* a la Las Vegas before Las Vegas. While a soldier in the French army, Martin started dreaming of expansive marble mansions. *Lucknow* lacks the stuff to materialize his dreams. Not to worry. With the nawab's blessings, Martin sets about replicating in brick what he fancies in marble. When the Nawab and his architect take breaks from building the massive collage that is *Lucknow*, they too enter cock fights with high stakes. Mir's ghazals can only fall on deaf ears. His jinxed rapport with *Lucknow* continues centuries after his death. I hear that his grave has disappeared. Perhaps they did not dig it deep enough.

Several degrees removed from this labyrinthine city, I am steadily losing my plot. My friend, Tausif, did not strive to study Urdu but it is he who runs an Urdu press from his house. *Taqreer* today does not have enough takers to justify the printing costs. Getting rid of the touch of paper maybe the sole remedy. What is stopping him from taking the electronic route is the unfairness of it all: readers who have sustained *Taqreer* so far might not be at ease with the internet. The move might alienate them. I keep assuring him that our language will not perish. I ask him to take heart from the fact that even in a distant country I have found people who revel in our Urdu and we have recruited quite a few members to our school's Urdu society. Yes, many members do not read the script but a language is much more than its script, isn't it? Ira, my world, my Lucknow, is found in Urdu. Yet the mirrors tell me, this is nothing but a reflection of that which I am yet to understand. How can I enter a reflection without shattering it? I can not return.

Love,
FZ

P.S: Your father's schedule in Delhi was packed and so was mine. We did not find the time to meet but a staff from his office delivered the package to me. It's huge. Do you mind if I open the package and distribute its contents across my bags to balance things out? He also sent a box of date palm jaggery sweets molded like swans. A very touching gesture on his part. Convey my regards to him.

5

The enlivened Durga pratima continues to haunt her. She can conjure that face a million times without its brilliance diminishing; and the blue veins that swelled on the fettler's wrist when he carved the deeper recesses around the idol's forehead! But after school, these days, all she does is tutor the neighbourhood children. She teaches math and history, subjects she does not care for but knows just about enough to help the class five students. How will she get through the difficult board examinations?

She envies her brother, whom Baba let drop out of school because during the season, which comes right in the middle of the academic year, family members need to oversee the work in their workshop. Baba asks, what good is education doing to the young boys in this city? They have not only made their own lives difficult but also augmented trouble for others. Schools and colleges remain closed for days at a stretch because of them. Their strikes will shut down factories. Consider how the police came up to his house even as his son had nothing to do with those rebels. The selfishness of those boys who put his wife's and daughter's lives at risk to save their own irks Baba. The perpetual fear of mob massacre has not done any good to his business. Baba hopes that his son will learn something more constructive through his apprenticeship at the workshop.

If you think you can run this business without knowing how to mould the idol with your own hands, then you are mistaken. It is god's work, the work of love. You ought to love this gift you have inherited. You can not run the workshop from the bamboo benches of the nearest tea stall. Do you really expect your labourers to take care of everything while you comfortably sit there and sip your tea? For them it is ultimately about their daily wage. You are the one in charge of the bigger picture, accountable for it. Besides, you will eventually need to train new boys and your own sons. Boys, who are on Baba's payroll for years, whom he trains with plenty of love and care, abandon him when they spot greener pastures. That's the way of the world and you need to brace yourself for it.

When she was younger, Baba did not mind her playing with clay. She could roll little clay balls between her warm palms. She could press those uneven wet orbs with her fingers to fashion swan's beaks. And, elephants, crows, or pairs of grooms and brides. The latter was somewhat exasperating. The task of crafting the bride's and the groom's bodies does not present many problems. But their faces! You should be able to tell the bride and the groom apart from their faces. That is the fundamental rule. Yet, how do you go about it? Both the dolls have spherical faces—not any larger than her favorite coconut ladoos. A problem of this magnitude warrants consultation with Baba. He, at the very least, has the benefit of experience. Baba is happy to share the secrets with her. What is more, with his nimble fingers Baba gives a demonstration—creates strands of hair for the bride and a squarish head, a side-parted hair as well as a moustache for the groom. She watched his fingers move with keen eyes, replicating it proximately with her astute hands.

But now she needs a good reason to enter the workshop. Sometimes she goes on the pretext of delivering lunches or conveying some message from Ma. Nobody would mind if she touched any of the models—technically, it all belongs to her family and to her. But a tacit agreement prompts her to stay away from the clay models. Couple of years back, when she was about to climb a stool to stick sweets between the lips of the Durga idol on the final day of the puja, Ma had stopped her. Gods will have nothing to do with leaky and messy girls like her. She had to wait another full year before she could greet the goddess. Entering Baba's workshop is like re-living that time of the month. What if an untimely drop of blood climbs down her thighs to soil the Durga pratima's neat saree or Ganesha's loin cloth?

While delivering lunch, she overhears two men debate the roundness desirable of an idol's belly. The hips of the idol ought to be motherly. But not so round as to seem as though she has just devoured a full meal of *hilsa* and a heap of rice so high that a cat can barely leap over it. Ganesha can be chubbier. He is the beloved younger son of Durga. But the contours of the childbearing waistlines of the ladies, Durga, Lakshmi, Saraswati, Kali ought to be watched. Do Baba and her brother think of the women they know—Ma and her—when they sculpt the goddesses? She remembers her younger, flat-chested body, stripped of clothes on the banks of the Hooghly, standing in her panties, watching the steamer packed with busy office-goers leave the jetty, before diving into the river—nakedness without guilt and the commonplace wonder of having the brown water, in which goddesses are routinely immersed, touch her skin, while a crow gets to rest on her clothes dangling from the steps of the ghat. Baba says the divinity of Kumartuli's idols result from their unlikeness to the real bodies and the real faces of women. If they let real women constrain their imagination, then wouldn't the Durga pratima end up looking like a bedecked doll? Her brother strides in, removing wax from his right ear with a bunch of keys.

What is she doing here?

She has brought lunch.

Keep it on the desk and go home.

Can't she stay?

No, Baba will be annoyed. Already the workshop lacks space. Today a worker tripped into a bucket of paint while climbing down a ladder that reached up to the goddess's shoulders. Even the idol seemed off balance for a few seconds, giving everyone a good scare. She will only add to the clutter.

But her brother can always tell Baba, whenever he returns, that she hasn't been around for very long.

Fine, but what will she do here? Her brother has to get work done.

She will quietly watch.

She asks one of the workers if she can help knead the clay. He laughs.

That year Baba contracts malaria. He shivers and pukes. He can not even stand on his own feet. The dampness left behind by the monsoon months impedes Baba's recovery. Even her brother keeps coughing at night. One afternoon, her brother brings his friends from the club and the tea stall to carry Baba down the stairs. They take Baba off to the hospital. Now it is Ma's and her duty to visit Baba there, every day. But there isn't much they can do. They sit next to him, wait for the doctor's errands to purchase medicines, and deliver home cooked meals. Baba needs the plainest of foods. Most often he can not even hold the food he eats for more than a few minutes. He throws up almost instantaneously after he has gulped a few morsels, even before the round and oblong antibiotics can be forced down his throat. Will he ever recover if he does not eat? How will his strength make its way back? Saline water trickles through a pipe stuck into his veins.

With Baba in the general ward of the hospital, a few miles away, no one regulates her entry into the workshop. For a family whose fortune is tied to the idol-making business, it is natural for her to help her brother while her father recovers, especially at this time of the year—the busy months leading up to the Durga Puja. But, of course, she is not here to oversee while others work. She wants to sculpt with her own hands, the way she used to carve the swans, elephants, brides, and grooms—the aspect of the craft that her Baba loves but rarely finds time for any more and that her brother does not enjoy. In order to sculpt the idol she has to work under the dwindling yellow light bulbs, alongside the men who bind the hay, knead the clay, sculpt, and deck the idols. She startles her brother with her keenness to work.

Given Baba's absence, her brother finally finds the respite to devote himself to get-rich-quick schemes. His card-playing companions have been an inspiration in this respect. However, he has also consistently hoped, with all his heart, for a sudden change of fate. When the wheel of fortune does turn, all he has to do is be on its right side. The tea seller assures him of his latent potential. And that too not just like that. The tea seller knows—he can read palms and has the much sought after gift of prescience. The astrologer who sits with a parrot near Ram Mandir is this tea seller's father. He has even greater powers. He had warned a man of his impending death under wheels. And to be sure the man came under a speeding bus the very next day and breathed his last even before the bus's wheels turned the corner. He had informed a woman that she would give birth to half a child. Nobody believed him, of course. How does anyone have half a child? But once again, sure enough the astrologer was right. The woman gave birth to a dwarf. Foretelling the future comes naturally to his son. Her brother often considered visiting this renowned and well-regarded astrologer. But since he had immediate access to this great man's son, he did not feel the acute need of consulting the father. The tea seller on his part let him know that he can depend on his fate and dream big.

His sister's interests baffle him. The hectic season before the pujas is no time to start learning. Does she not know that boys are recruited earlier in the year so that they may contribute efficiently by this point? But can't she at least roll the clay to carve simple things like the fingers and the fists of the idols? Or perhaps help define the contours of the idol's faces, barely cast, lying in the sun along the door of the workshop? Why do all the idols in their workshop have identical clay faces year after year? Same eyes, same nose, same chin, same lips. Baba says each family of idol-makers has its own style. Very well. But why should this familial style never change?

Most men in the workshop are suspicious of her. When she walks past the idols, tucking the loose ends of the saree around her waist, they half expect a few models to topple. But she is yet to wreak any havoc for them to formally rise in revolt. Now she is about to leave for the evening. She has to reach the hospital in time for the visiting hours, after making sure her hands or clothes don't give away where she has been all day.

Cool water from the blue jug glides along her elbow to the

floor. A silhouette walks toward her—no, walks past her. The silhouette has a bag on his shoulders and seems to know his way around. Yes, it is him. No doubt about that. Why is that man with the mole, which looks like a nose stud, entering their workshop? He has the same perplexing face that she had seen, drawn, and dreamed.

Look at Bhola's sister going for an evening stroll with her husband. The amount of vermilion she has put in the parting of her hair could fill a little box. How beautiful and radiant she looks. Must have put on some weight post-wedding. Her toe ring catches the twilight. Her heels lined with auspicious red paint peep from under the sari's borders that end slightly above her ankles. Bhola's sister had eloped with the man who is walking beside her now, holding her hand. The man with that stray lock of hair curled on his forehead—Uttam Kumar! They had exchanged garlands in front of the goddess Kali in the temple at Kalighat.

Don't you know that Bhola's father wanted to marry her—his youngest daughter—into a family that would also offer their daughter's hand to Bhola? He was ready to pay a handsome dowry to facilitate that transaction. But Bhola found no bride. How long could the younger sister wait for a miracle to happen in her brother's life? As soon as she found someone reliable, she eloped with him, in plain clothes, without even a crow hearing of her plans until it had been successfully executed. People widely believed that her parents would never see her or the guy's faces again. They were that angry. Her father had even filed a report with the police. But look at them now. Bhola's parents even prepared elaborate meals with nine side dishes for the groom on Jamai Shashti. As customs dictate, Bhola's mother sits next to her son-in-law while he eats, swinging a handheld fan.

The man with the mole is at work early next morning. He has climbed a stool ladder to smoothen the shoulders of the idol with a flat, wet brush. The red and brown checked shirt he wore last evening hangs on the door. His clavicle forces itself against his dark skin. The hair on his chest bursts through the holes of his sweat-stained cotton gunjee. How had she never seen him before at the workshop? He is this year's new recruit who specialises in drawing the idol's eyes, her brother informs her. He had got a week's leave because of a crisis in his family. He is not much of a talker. When he does talk, his voice can hardly be heard above the surrounding noise, which includes honking cars, tinkling rickshaw bells, the hammering of nails, and high-pitched hoots of men calling out to one another. Soon she finds that he is not much of an eater either. He does not have lunch or tea. Perhaps he has taken some kind of a vow before his favourite gods. Who knows? As long as he gets the work done, does it matter whether he eats or fasts? His toe nails are the colour of clay. Four thin lines mark the corner of his eyes when he concentrates on some of the finer details of the idols. After days of observing from a distance, she approaches him. She will learn from him.

Three weeks later, Baba returns home but he is not yet fit for the workshop. He is lacking in appetite and strength. Ma is tired of feeding him and cleaning buckets filled to the brim with his sour vomit. Meanwhile, she continues to have her way. Albeit now she can only visit the workshop during school hours. Does Baba know what she has been up to while he was gone? Nobody seems to openly discuss her activities with Baba. Not even her uncle who has seen her at the workshop more than once. Like her, they know whatever she sculpts in clay will not take too long to dissolve in Hooghly.

Baba's health is improving, thank god for that. But he

will soon take over. He will not let her spend time at the workshop. When he finds out that she has not been attending school, he will cane her. Blood rushes to her cheeks and ears when she ominously pictures Baba catching her clay-handed. Sometimes while fettling layers of clay from the idol's arms, she feels a pair of eyes look over her shoulders. She half expects it to be Baba.

Playing "*Aro Dure Cholo Jai*", a band party marches past the workshop. Must be a wedding or some puja procession. She is grateful for the festivities around these lanes that never seem to draw to a close. She turns. The man with the mole has been keenly following her work. He joins her hand to affirm her grip on the chisel and slices the air with ever expanding circular movements. Everyone else, including her brother, deals with her in the manner in which she deals with her younger cousins during the hide and seek games. But the man with the mole hands her his own brushes and chisel. Her brother never learned that she brought lunch for this man secretly in the same steel tiffin carrier used to fetch Baba's lunch; that she was initially disappointed when he did not touch the food but relieved as he promised to have that cold, hard rice at night.

Time for delivery of the idols. Few idols receive their last-minute touches. The lanes are bustling with customers, carts to carry the idols, labourers, artists, middlemen. One of Baba's loyal customers, from the Jogeshwari park puja organisers, has come to take the idol they had commissioned for their pandal. The Jogeshwari puja has had a longstanding relationship with their workshop. Even when Baba's father was at the helm of the business, the Jogeshwari committee would take their idol from this house. The familiar Durga goddess, wrapped in her clay saree painted red with golden borders, stares down at the evil muscular demon, Mahishashura. Baba offers tea to his customers. The tea seller will stay up tonight for the brisk business. The customers attempt to negotiate some costs which have been added at the last minute. Baba argues that he hardly has any margin of profit. Bhakti Poddar, one of the old timers from Jogeshwari, has his eyes fixated on the idol's face. Something about the face of the idol strikes him as unusual. The Banarasi pan masala's buzz is not strong enough to mess with his sight. He keeps scanning the idol's visage. The mystery needs to be solved before he can put his mind to anything else.

Does Bhakti da want another cup of tea?

His wife has urged him to cut down on the number of cups. So only one more cup. That's it. Final cup for the night.

The idol's chin has a distinct cleft, less than an inch in length but deep, as if the clay from the rounded chin has been fettled with a delicate knife. Hardly noticeable in itself, the cleft cuts across the composure of the idol's demeanor. This face no longer belongs in calendars or petrified statues. He looks around. All the idols in the workshop have the cleft in their chin—each blending into the other, distinct yet diffused. He hopes to see that cleft year after year.

Before the next season, she failed her higher secondary board examinations. Fortunately, she had been appeasing Lord Shiva by pouring milk and water over his linga and fasting through Shiva ratri. Shiva is, as you know, in charge of getting young girls married to husbands like himself—suitable candidates with minor flaws such as addiction to pot, fiery temper, and very rarely, a proclivity for adultery. Ma got Baba through her devotion to Lord Shiva, alongside, of course, at least ten other gods. One can never be too careful about these things. So, Baba is not exactly like Shiva. On her part, she would much rather consent to marrying someone like Kartik than Shiva but the former does not accept prayers to that effect. For good measure, this past year, she had even nagged her brother to take her to the Charak celebrations where saints clad in saffron with ash on their forehead displayed miraculous, athletic feats following their month of penance in honour of Shiva. The props of the saints included tridents, drums, knives, and fire. They jumped from trees onto sharp knives, inspiring awe in onlookers like her. Shiva shielded these men, his devotees, from material harm.

So, after her failure in the exams, when Saraswati deserted office, Shiva swiftly filled the vacancy and took matters into his own hands. She was married off to the owner of a sweet shop in another part of the city. The wedding was a small-scale affair. The whole thing happened smoothly. The only hiccup was that the groom's decorated white ambassador could not enter the lanes leading to her house, which was the wedding venue. Even while leaving, the morning after the wedding, the bride and the groom had to board a hand-pulled rickshaw before they reached the broader street from where the rented ambassador picked them up.

Almost two hundred guests attended the reception thrown from the groom's side. Her in-laws own the old shop well known for the exquisite sweets made from fresh jaggery, moulded into various shapes: conch shells, huts, fish, crows. That year, during the Bijoya festivities, they sold a limited edition coconut crusted sweet moulded as a Durga pratima: the familiar betel leaf shaped face of the goddess with elongated eyes, delicately protruding nose with a giant nose ring and a minuscule cleft in her chin. The outer crust was hard while on the inside the sweet was soft and chewy, melting in your mouth before you knew it.

6

Search: *Metiaburj*
Tuesday, 28 May 2013
1:32 AM

from: Fasahat Zaidi <zaidi.fasahat@h-mail.com>
to: ira.chatterjee12@h-mail.com

This morning I dreamed that I came to visit you in Kolkata. We cavorted around your Kumartuli lanes. You wanted to stop and look at the picture gallery of an abandoned mansion across a cemented courtyard but I thought it was ugly. Instead, we found a small shack, where I could order us a cup of tea, in Bengali. Then we drowned in Hooghly, briefly, only to surface at some distance from a steamer. Its black whistles were easy to hear from under the water. But damp locks blocked your line of sight. Gasping for breath, you asked me how much further we had to go. The vessel was closing in, fast.

On the upper deck of the steamer, the deceased actor Amjad Khan sat aplomb on a diwan in full regalia, surrounded by women—he called the women "paris." We recognized them as the stars of the legendary Rahas that had premiered on the Shahi stage. That show had not lasted very long despite its grand opening. You and I had hoped to catch the performance that followed Rahas' success—Mian Amanat's *Inder Sabha*—the first theatrical production in Urdu, executed by these paris. But we were late on our way into deep memory. There had been detours. We had stumbled across doors that were actually dead ends and reached the show after curtain call. Now we had the entire cast on the other side of the water-eaten rails of the steamer.

Snatches of thumri in Pt. Bhimsen Joshi's voice were comforting us even as we shivered in the cold water. Nonetheless, I tried to keep time, as poets should. The steamer was also a floating zoo. Pigeons, quails, and parrots fluttered in cages. Cheetahs and cows, rams and rhinoceroses drank water from the same end of the vessel. Finally a woman gave us her hand. A pari herself no doubt, she sparkled in a teal blue pishwa with silver ornaments on her arms and a maroon dot on her forehead. Her stooped body guarded the descending sun. Whiffs of attar welcomed us aboard. Thank god, you said, we did not give up so close to the nest. The woman withdrew from our company and joined a group of turbaned men. When the steamer came ashore, the travelers beheld the approaching land. The woman announced, 'this dome we see after our Shah is named mud,' that is *Metiaburj*. You and I did not risk offending anyone and so we merely chuckled but the entourage broke out in immoderate laughter. Even Amjad Khan—the exiled Awadhi Nawab who would die in Kolkata after recording the nuances of ragas and bols in lithographs. By the time we reached dry land, all the trains were gone. A rickshaw puller offered us a ride, though we did not have rupees to pay him. Overhearing our conversation about the odd crew who had rescued us, the rickshaw puller, to our astonishment, claimed to have descended from the woman, actually a man: Gustakh. But our state was out of its wits. So Gustakh's descendant pulled the rickshaw instead of our leg.

I woke up in silence. The obituary to everything is wordlessness. Now I hear myself exhale softly, blowing an orphan strand of hair, coiled in a reluctant semi-circle, caught between the leaves of that book you gifted. When did you outgrow the purple highlights? Another day, it could have been Rizwan in my dream in your place. Today though, I am thinking of the night when we spotted each other. We could be friends, I thought. But then, you brought up Rizwan. Whenever I read the poem I dedicate to him, I recount a few anecdotes before the audience. The more I told the stories, the more I was certain to own them. The Rizwan of my anecdotes was always travelling with me, growing in my mind, and my mind alone. Your words fractured that Rizwan. As you started, "hey, what a coincidence, I have this friend called Rizwan who's also in Delhi…," I wished you would halt, allow laughter to take over, and let the moment slip. Instead you chased down every last bit of him. I had left Rizwan behind, I had left Tausif behind. They wanted too much of me. Simply writing and publishing poems and running an Urdu society isn't what they thought I would amount to when they resuscitated me. Yes, there was a time when they did everything to ensure I lived and breathed, thought and wrote. I failed them. Ran to this continent. Then you came along smiling, tipping a glass of single malt scotch on my kurta and the story took a new turn. I want to play the polyamorous poet, Ira, except I can't. It's like running both to and from my own memory and no matter how hard I run and which way I go, I will be late.

And being late is hardly figurative given the state of affairs in my life. I have broken yet another deadline. I could not bring myself to submit to the Irving chapbook competition because I know that these are not the poems I promised myself when I took up the residency. I am hundreds of words away from anything worth sharing but the clock is ticking. Here Abbu and Ammi ask me when I will be back for good and what job I will get. On the terrace of a house, I had once tried to tell them who I was but it is as though my words never reached their ears. I might go to Delhi this weekend. It's been a year since I have seen Rizwan.

Love,
Zaidi

Wednesday, 29 May 2013
05:17 PM

from: ira.chatterjee12@h-mail.com
to: Fasahat Zaidi <zaidi.fasahat@h-mail.com>

Zaidi, you know, I have a thing or two to say about *Metiaburj*. I'm sure you have Riz on your mind. That's why the dream! Riz hasn't been to *Metiaburj* in years, of course, and here in our Midwestern la-la-land much has happened over the last few days and I am drained. I don't know if you'd noticed (Oh sorry, that's a rhetorical question because nothing escapes Zaidi's eyes!), Clara had a mole just below the shoulder on her back. I took it to be a birth mark and never asked Amby about it. Amby, on the other hand, thought that it's acne, which would go away. Late Sunday night, Clara complained of a painful sensation on her back. Amby wasn't there and her roomie was looking after Clara. She eventually gave Clara a painkiller but Clara immediately threw up. Finally when Amby got back from work, Clara had recovered a bit. So they stay put for the night. I didn't even know any of this until I got a call early Monday morning.

Clara had been admitted to the ER of the university hospital by that point because the pain had returned. When I managed to visit, the doctors had taken Clara to run some tests on her. Amby was holding up fine. Her roomie had taken off from work and was with her. I had to leave to cover my recitation section and then I had a meeting scheduled with Dr Harris about the state of my research question (fyi: currently, she doesn't think that my thesis about female idol-makers, without having found one, is going anywhere, and I can't blame her, but I have got in touch with the Mritsilpi Samity, that is the Idol-makers' Union, and they claim to have all sorts of records, so I am hopeful about getting some leads). When I returned in the evening I felt super guilty for having left Amby. That acne thing was a tumor!! Who would have thunk it? Clara needed immediate surgery. What's more, the doctors suspected the tumor to be malignant.

And, meanwhile, Amby wasn't certain what costs would be covered by her and Clara's insurance company. So, it was ugly. Amby is tough as nails, you and I know that. She has been raising Clara on her own, never as much as mentioning that asshole who left her pregnant. She was on the phone with the insurance people for at least an hour. Though distressed, she was blasting Macklemore through her headset and that's what made it scarier. Clara was freaked out from just being in the hospital. She hated the smell (no idea what the smell was, none of us breathed anything out of the ordinary). Then, Amby's parents came down from California late that night.

Had they not assured Amby that they could help her with the co-pay, I can't imagine what would have happened.

The surgery was successfully performed yesterday and the tumor was benign. Thank god. Just when we thought all would be well, the pediatric surgeon in charge began to grill Amby, demanding to know how she had let the tumor grow as much. While admitting Clara, Amby had honestly recounted the symptoms of the night before. It was on file and this peds person wanted to know why she waited a night before bringing Clara to the hospital. One thing led to another and suddenly, out of nowhere, after the successful surgery, this lady decided that a clinical social worker should be called to discuss Amby's "family issues"! Nothing Amby or we said would convince this doctor to act otherwise. That Clara's single, working mother takes adequate care of her was beyond this ped doc's reckoning. You had to see the way she spoke to Amby. Scathing! She wouldn't stop reminding Amby of the responsibilities that come with motherhood. It was heartbreaking, you know, Zaidi. Whatever Amby does is for Clara. We know that. The overtimes, the night shifts, the stuff after school. I'm sure deep inside Amby was already blaming herself more than the doctors ever would for not bringing Clara in earlier. Amby and her family spent hours convincing the doctors that Clara is taken care of. It's sad when you have to do something like that in front of others.

So, despite the successful surgery, we spent a long sleepless night on the benches of the hospital. Amby had not consumed anything all day, except youtube videos on parotid tumors. At midnight, when she finally agreed to have some food, there was nothing to be found except the junk in the vending machine. That's when we saw your doctor-friend Andrew (who, according to Amby, looks like the actor playing Jesse

Pinkman on *Breaking Bad*). I didn't recognize him when he said hi. Then he reminded me that we had met twice, once at Bodega and then at Rustoroma. He was telling me that he saw you before you left for India. I told him that we are moving in together after you get back. Clearly, your urologist can't get enough of you...lol. What do you boys do during your frequent visits? :-o. I'm glad we bumped into the guy though. He said he'll also keep himself abreast of Clara's case. Hopefully he can do something to keep the social workers at bay. The peds doctor has to stop threatening that they can take Clara away from Amby.

I'll try to get some sleep now. And, Z, please be a little more strategic about using the time you have in India. You told me that your funding will run out in a year and it takes forever to edit, send out the manuscript, and get it published. If you don't have another fellowship or some such appointment by this time next year, then how will you sustain yourself? (I don't believe I am the one giving you advice about time management given what I am doing with my research, but for what it's worth, we both need to get our shit together.) And, on a very different note, I don't think we should try to find a roommate for the room in the basement. Amby needs some space to work, where she can sketch her (pro-bono) models like me (!). So, let her have the basement. I wouldn't want her to pay us. She can share the utilities maybe. What do you think?

Ira

Thursday, 30 May 2013
03:17 AM

from: Lavanya Chatterjee <chatterjeelavanya@h-mail.com>
to: ira.chatterjee12@h-mail.com

dear ira,
hope the little girl you babysit is doing better. i imagine what
amber must be going through. blood, surgeries scare me and
even more so, if it is you under the knife. when you were small,
every time you caught some disease my heart sink. if you were
in pain, i started to cry. one time you had fever for five days at
a stretch. no matter what medicine the doctor gave, the fever
wouldn't subside. your father and i could not eat or sleep.
every few minutes we check your temperature in the hopes
that it would go down. now that you are so far away, whenever
your voice sounds cracked on the phone, i think of you as the
child in my arms, suffering from something mysterious. i feel
helpless and that's how all parents feel when children suffer.
    children, on the other hand, are different. when i sneeze
and sneeze because of the scented candles you light up in
the house, you do not seem to care. and now your father is
following your footsteps. the candles and room fresheners
remind him of you. he bought a new one, which smells like
rotting night jasmine. your father believes it emits a sweet
and fresh fragrance. his nose must be blocked. i send him
to buy flour and the grocerywala sees his chance. he pushes
your father to buy these things. i can say with confidence, no
one else would buy it but your father. every shopkeeper in
this locality knows how lenient you and your father are in all
money matters and they take full advantage of it. your father
especially. he haggles for the price of a needle but purchases

a useless elephant without second thought. how totally sick i feel when dousing my house with artificial fragrances!

i write to you not to complain of my illness but to say something else, which is more important. you're a grown up now but, ira, you need to understand that every time your father and i prevent you from doing something, it is because we care. on phone today when you brought up our attempts to keep you from visiting rizwan in *metiaburj*, and accused us again of being intolerant, etc., i thought this girl will never learn anything and that is why i forget to tell you about my application. don't you know, not too long ago *metiaburj* was in news again? bombs were found stocked in houses there after a blast killed several people. consider now how you argued with us when your father and i suggested, you don't go to that locality by yourself. without ever stepping into *metiaburj*, you become its champion. according to you, your parents are mostly wrong. and that rizwan also, just like you, argues with his parents. he hasn't made amends with them, has he? it's not easy for parents to accept that their child did not turn out alright. i know i know you think being gay is normal and i accept your ideas and friends but i would be shocked too if you were gay, even though i am so open-minded that i watched *my brother nikhil* first day first show. the muslims are more conservative, so it is not surprising that rizwan's parents reacted, more violently. rizwan should have apologized to them. instead he severed all ties. that's not how parents deserve to be treated but none of you get it.

and here is the important thing: you need to write an application for me today. i e-mail you the flyer of a conference about hindustani music. see. i want to participate in it. you type the application and resume for me. i would ask your father to do that but he is already swamped with office work and when he comes back he has to help me with the chores because malati our newest domestic help has left. even when she was working, she was looking for excuses to remain absent. today this, tomorrow that. this time she left to celebrate shib gajan and never returned, not even to take her pending salary! she said someone from her family would perform feats at the charak mela. it has become difficult to keep servants in this house! going to america, at least you have learnt to do your own work yourself. so when you return you won't need servants. that is a very good thing in times of crisis like this. now don't forget about my application.

Ma

Sunday, 2 June 2013
11:30 AM

from: ira.chatterjee12@h-mail.com
to: Fasahat Zaidi <zaidi.fasahat@h-mail.com>

Zaidi, that was a summer of unceasing nor'westers. The lane in front of our house remained blocked for days. The unruly summer winds had uprooted a huge neem tree. While falling, the tree drilled a massive hole in the roof of a workshop and smashed a host of unsold Saraswati idols. You know, I had once damaged the Saraswati idol kept in our house by throwing a tape recorder at it and mom had flinched saying, it will bring a curse on our family. Perhaps the neem tree brought a curse on our city, Kolkata. Mom and I were watching a repeat telecast of the Rabindra Jayanti celebration on Doordarshan. The cable channels were down. Even as the women danced in yellow sarees, with flame-of-the-forest blooms tucked in their buns, and men in khadi kurtas beat the tabla, scrolling marquees flashed headlines about this one woman from Bihar who had won the prestigious Gutzwiller Prize for her debut collection of Urdu poetry. Meanwhile, a group of children moved on to sing praises of the fire kindled by music.

In the 7 PM news, we watched reporters make their way through the small town (more like village) of Saleempara to bring us a glimpse of this girl in her mid-twenties touted as the nation's next literary gem. Fatima Ali did not come out of her single-story flat roof house to claim her fifteen minutes of fame but her father did, only to inform us about his daughter's refusal to engage with any reporters. That was that. We would forget all about this poet if not for a TV channel's desperate attempt at making sure that its coverage of Ali's maiden international triumph was different from those of the other channels. A couple of days after the news of her award had run its course, the channel—24/7 News—aired a 15-minute special. They hadn't been able to get hold of the poet. No surprises there. But they had managed to bring in some experts to weigh in on the merits of her poetry.

I hadn't watched the 24/7 News show when it was first aired but learned of it when a newspaper picked up something said on the show as a headline for its front page. In the collection of poems that had won Gutzwiller, Ali had apparently compared the formless Allah with eunuchs (though, as Riz would later explain to me, if one read past the enjambment, one would realize that Ali had actually written that eunuchs had Allah's grace or something like that). The experts on 24/7 News were two carefully curated politicians: one from a right-wing Hindu party, which was the primary political opposition in the Madhuban district at the time, and the other, the elected MP of the region, who did not spare opportunities to remind his audience that he was a staunch Sunni Muslim, who abided by the words of Allah and Allah alone. The host of the show summed up the gist of the poems and then asked the experts' opinions. The host's summary was the source of next day's newspaper headline. The MP decided that the international recognition was actually an American conspiracy in the aftermath of 9/11. It was no coincidence that America applauded such anti-Islam poems. In the coverage that followed, we learned bits and pieces of information about Fatima Ali. She received her primary education at a Madrasa until the headmaster there issued a circular making the campus girl-free, because he decided that co-education is against the spirit of Islam. Ali's father then enrolled her in a school in an adjacent town. She got a BA degree in English from a college in Patna. According to her schoolteachers, she was an extraordinary student and a polyglot. She was adept in Urdu, Hindi, Bengali, Bhojpuri, and English. Some claimed she also knew Arbi and Farsi. Ali herself never gave any bytes and eventually, despite the scintillating headlines, the media lost interest in her. Even when a fatwa was issued against her, the news did not make it to the front pages.

By then, summer had turned into monsoon. I had to wade through knee-high pools of water after getting out of the metro station to reach college. Travelling by car was no longer an option given that it would take hours to get anywhere because of the traffic jams. Riz had not come to college for 3–4 days. It wasn't alarming. The weather was bad and attendance was low. However, during a conversation with the head of our department, Ashwin learned that Riz had broken his leg and so, would remain absent for a while. Riz did not have a cellphone, you know. I mean, it was before we had smartphones and such but all of us, at least, had cellphones. Riz found it intrusive. You know what I mean. So, we always had to call his landline. Anyway, we just decided that we would pay a surprise visit and bring him all the college gossip and notes. There was one minor hiccup though. None of us had been to his house or knew where he lived. Sometimes after classes, he would come with me in my car and ask to be dropped at Park Circus. That's all we had to go by in order to guess where he lived. While it would have been adventurous to locate his residence on our own (though I don't know how we would have done that), we decided to enlist the help of the head of our department and he handed Riz's address to us.

Riz, to our surprise, lived not in Park Circus but in *Metiaburj*. Sneha did not even know where *Metiaburj* was. Ashwin and I had a vague idea about its location. To Ashwin it was the place where his brothers went to buy kites. In terms of distance, it wasn't far removed from central Kolkata but it was out of our radar. Yet, we decided to go see him. I brought up the subject with Mom-Dad because I thought dad could offer better directions to get to the place. What happened though was that Mom refused to let me go there because apparently it was a terrible, unsafe area. I assured her that Sneha and Ashwin would come along. This information had the contrary effect. Mom immediately called Sneha's parents to tell her about our impending life-threatening journey. Mom at her most bizarre. So then far from getting the right directions, I was told that I couldn't visit a friend because my parents were paranoid. Surprisingly, Sneha agreed with her (and my) parents and Ashwin said that he couldn't go because he had to catch up with work, leaving me to my own means.

The rains ensured my parents wouldn't send the car with our driver to pick me up. After college, I asked around for buses to take to *Metiaburj* but got confused by the myriad directions I was getting. So, I cabbed. It was late in the evening and after some difficulty I located Riz's house. I thought Riz would be thrilled to see me but first he was aghast, then, furious. He taunted me for saying it was difficult to come to his place. I kid you not when I say that he was sort of jumping and going, little Ira lost her way. hee haw hee haw...Miss Ira jumped on her chariot excitedly, rehearsing the few words of consolation meant for her friend with a broken leg... Awww (making faces).... Her friend would return her welling eyes with welling eyes, she was confident... Awww.... Tenderness would know no bounds, except she had the wrong address.

He can be such a douche sometimes. Part of it must have been that he was not very comfortable about me finding out where he lived—he called it the 'bushy rear of the city of joy'. He had several relatives living in the same house with his family and I don't know if it bothered him that they saw me. His mother was welcoming. But, by then, I was feeling nauseous anticipating my parents' reaction once they learned where I had come. I wasn't much of a rebel, you see. Knowing that Mom would start calling me in some time, I switched off my cellphone. Riz was not even grateful that I got him notes from the class but after I emerged from the loo he became more sympathetic. He mentioned what was really bothering him: Fatima Ali's house in Saleempara had been torched by a mob the previous night. Her parents and two younger siblings had been burned alive!! Ali herself had left for Patna earlier that fateful evening and narrowly escaped what was clearly a pre-meditated attack on her life. Riz and I had never discussed Ali before that evening. I had no clue that Riz had been collecting bits and pieces of her poems from little magazines and newspaper clips about her from the time she won the Gutzwiller. The other candidate to take interest in Ali's career was Bengal's Chief Minister. The next day he publicly announced that Bengal is this secular seat of art and culture and if Bihar was not being able to protect a young poet, Bengal would. Ali could come and stay in Kolkata and the state would protect her from extremist hooligans.

No one could protect me from my parents though. To say that they were mad at me is an understatement. My mother was convinced that I had plans of eloping with Riz, which was especially ironic given that Riz had come out to me as gay (much before coming out to his family) and I had told my mom about it. Mom was of the opinion that no one can be really gay. It is a phase, which people eventually get over, and when Riz had had enough of gaiety, we would run off together. The other dramatic plot on her mind was that Riz would turn me gay (and this still haunts her since I am around you; bisexual and gay are all basically the same orientation for Mom). Mom-Dad asked me to stay away from Riz but their threats and warnings were mostly idle because, you know, they didn't really do anything to stop me from hanging out with Riz.

Riz came back to college in time and Ali also made her way to Kolkata I suppose, because around mid-September there was this massive rally stalling the traffic in Esplanade demanding the CM throw her out of the city and ban her books. One of the university presses in Kolkata, sponsored by the state, had decided to publish a new edition of her award-winning chapbook in order to make it available for wider audiences. Some thugs wouldn't have it and a copyeditor of the press, a post-graduate student himself, lodged an FIR against a group of strangers who roughed him up on his way to the university campus. It was a peculiar year, the way I remember it. Earlier, there had been a series of bandhs because a Muslim guy was allegedly killed by the family of his Hindu lover and the same group that had risen up against the state government for siding with the influential family of the Hindu girl, were up in arms against Ali and the government's decision to shelter her. Dad used to follow the coverage of these rallies and protests, nod his head, and say that this is not the Kolkata he had known and lived in all his life. He was very young when the Naxal movement had taken over the city and recalled everything that happened after, including the emergency, as a largely peaceful era. Riz on the other hand believed that this was the culmination of something he had known for a long time. You see, Dad, Mom, Riz, everyone had an opinion. Even Ashwin once chimed in, out of nowhere, about Bengali Hindus being particularly intolerant and discriminating of Marwaris. I was the least opinionated among the people I knew. And when each of them spoke, I saw their point. However, they would not get one another: like when I told Riz what Dad said about Kolkata, he said that it was the complacency of families like ours that had driven Kolkata to where it was. It was the first time he had made that distinction between my world and his, something that he does all the time now.

During class, instead of taking notes, Riz would doodle in his notebook. He told me he couldn't stop thinking about this woman, merely a few years older than us, who had lost everything but her life for writing poems. We knew so little of her and yet her figure overshadowed the late evening jam sessions we had next to the back gate of our college. Ashwin was planning a career in music those days, one that he never pursued, thank god, and would bring his guitar to college. The guitar, as opposed to his voice, never failed to score points with women.

A week ahead of the Durga Puja vacations, Riz proposed we perform a street play on the college premises and follow it up with a discussion with the audience. The play was to address the tension simmering in the aftermath of Fatima Ali's supposed arrival in the city. Riz's bright idea was to adapt one of her long narrative poems into a play. Mind you, apart from Riz, none of us read Urdu. He volunteered to act as the liaison between the poem and us. Sneha and I were the default scriptwriters of our group. We had presented skits for college fests and even won prizes as a team. So, the proposal wasn't completely out of order but the lofty ends that Riz was after were clearly unattainable. He thought of the play as an act of resistance. To me it was yet another excuse to hang with the gang after college hours. But, in order to realize his goals, Riz insisted that we don't seek permission from our college and burst into the performance on the college compound, taking passers by completely by surprise, and in the end, ask them where they stood on the persecution of Ali and the possibility of bans imposed on her. No points for guessing I wasn't on board with Riz's suggestion.

Our college maintained an apolitical stance about everything. They were all about discipline. We had student unions and it was an open secret that these were supported by different political factions, but we pretended that anything going on behind the walls of the college was of no consequence outside and vice-versa. Our college authorities were not okay with us wearing clothes of our choice (really!) and I knew that they would take us to task for performing the play and bringing the ongoing political clamor into the campus. On the other hand, if we sought permission for a play enforcing abstract ideals that both our college and country set for themselves—freedom of expression—then it would go down fine. We just had to pretend it wasn't about what it was about, though we all knew better. It was a simple enough job: remove some specifics from the script, avoid direct references to Ali (maybe not even mention that her poems were the basis of the script), and bring the dean on board. But that was unacceptable to Riz. He believed that we should not only avoid any dissemblance but also congratulate ourselves if the play prompted any kneejerk reaction from the college administration. I'm sure you know that he could be foolhardy like that.

We worked on the composition at my place that weekend. The ban on Riz had been unofficially lifted by Mom and Dad. Mom even cooked an eggplant dish that Riz loves. All that was great but I was anxious. I knew better than to tell my parents by that point. So, I decided to go ahead and seek permission from our dean, without informing Riz and the others. I rehearsed the script I would blurt out in front of the dean: it's a street play exalting human rights of expression and so on. All would be well. My appraisal was on point for once. The dean immediately consented. As literature students, he said, we were on the right track. He was all for encouraging art on campus. But. Since we were planning to perform on the college compound during a break, when the basketball team practised there, he believed we should talk to the principal or vice-principal about it as well. Before I could reflect on the matter and say that we could perform anywhere really and it didn't have to be the compound, I found myself standing in front of our vice-principal's office, alongside the dean. The VP had a million questions. Why, who, what, when and my euphemistic answers wouldn't have got me very far but the dean intervened. He backed me up and so, in the end, the VP let us have our way.

And thus my fears were put to rest. The D-day was a Thursday, a day before the last class. The play was in rhyming couplets, in English, mirroring the original Urdu poems. We looked hardcore in black t-shirts, blue jeans, and red dupattas around our waists. I also had a piece of black cloth around my eyes as per Riz's direction. You know, the thing about street plays is that your turf is a blank slate before you begin. You fill it with syllables and movements of your throbbing body, expecting the tempo to resonate with the strangers. After all, they have the same ground beneath their feet. Then you begin to feel the havoc that blood and breath are wreaking in your body and you forget to wish that the audience don't walk away, and they don't.

We were about ten minutes into the play when the VP tore through the assembled audience. The officers of the student union were behind him. As representatives of the student body, the officers said they objected to the subject matter of the play. The VP demanded we discontinue the production. Riz protested that the officers could not object because they hadn't been there to watch it. One of them, Sushant, retaliated, claiming that I told them all about the script. Of course, I hadn't told them or anyone anything, apart from the VP and the dean, but they insisted that they had it from me! Riz punched Sushant, someone hurled a stone at us from behind the gathered crowd, and that's how it started. In a few minutes the site had transformed into a scuffle field of sorts. We were tugging and hitting one another. Guards and cops were called to restrain us. Even as faculty remained divided over the next course of action, a bunch of people gathered in front of our college. They were calling for the suspension of the students who had threatened the secular campus run on tax payers' money with an anti-Islam show.

Subsequently, the VP threatened to file charges against us for provoking violence on campus. Before Dad came to talk to the principal and extract us from the college premises that evening, we were sitting in an empty classroom. It was not just Riz, Ashwin, Sneha, and me but a host of other students, some of whom we did not even know. We had minor cuts here and there and my ankle had twisted while trying to escape the mob. Riz wasn't even looking at me (let alone talking) because of my supposed betrayal. When Dad came, Riz initially refused to leave with us. But Dad insisted. A curfew was supposed to start in an hour. Once in the car, Dad told us that Riz should stay at our place that night. Apparently, the fights on campus were not the only ones of the sort that afternoon. Stray incidents of violence had occurred in several pockets of the city. The unfolding events and their live coverage came to a head when some hooligans shattered a news channel's van parked near our college campus, while another mob went door to door looking for Fatima Ali in Park Circus. So when Dad learned about our situation he couldn't come at once. Main roads in the city were jammed. Mobs were setting fire to houses, shops, and cars in areas they suspected Fatima Ali to be hiding. The police resorted to using tear gas to contain the crowd in Park Circus and *Metiaburj*. Once Riz heard this, he was no longer prepared to come over with us. He left for his place and god knows how he got there with no buses running.

As our car sped through the city, I noted the state of the roads. I had seen deserted roads during bandhs but this was different. The central avenue looked like an empty bed from which a corpse had just been lifted. The curfew didn't restore order either. That night a faceless mass brought down the near-complete Durga Puja pandal in Park Circus and another irreparably damaged the workshop of a sculptor in

Metiaburj. Rakib Chacha, as Riz knew this sculptor, carved Hindu gods on the ground floor of his own house. Riz used to mention the sculptor's singular face: there was a mole on his nose which looked like a black diamond stud. He didn't sculpt idols for worship though he had worked in Kumartuli when he was younger. The idols he produced were small, with detailed inlay work, commissioned by people as decorations for their houses. Some clients provided him with raw materials like ivory and sandalwood. Over the years several factions had tried to evict him from the area but ordinary people, his neighbors, always came out in his support. Riz's brother was one of the people who formed a human chain in front of Rakib Chacha's house to prevent the mob from attacking him and his family the next morning.

Riz did not speak to me for several months and when he did, he informed me that Fatima Ali was forced to flee Kolkata because of what happened. By that point, Riz either believed that I hadn't meant to betray him even when I had gone behind his back or that none of what happened was up to me or any of us; yet, we were never on the same terms again. Next year, he left for Delhi and our conversations became infrequent. I did not hear that he had come out to his parents and that his brother had whacked him and flung him outside the house until much later. Now Riz asks me to forget about Fatima Ali and about all that happened. I had forgotten in a sense, but you know, the more I interact with Riz and you these days, the more I think of her but for no particular reason. Maybe my search for the female idol-maker whom no one knows of reminds me of Ali because she was always out of sight, before disappearing completely. How do some people go off the grid? If I wanted to leave everything and disappear right now, I am certain I would be found. Whatever, I'll go see Amby now. Clara is out of the hospital. There are too many people looking after Clara for the time being but Amby is very shaken by the experience. You should call or write to her, Z. Take care.

Ira

7

Sunday, 14 July 2013
08:45 AM

from: Sumit Chatterjee <chat.sumit1@fas.mail.org>
to: ira.chatterjee12@h-mail.com

Dearest Ira,

When do I get to see you again? In my memory you are still a high school kid. But young lady, you will soon become a doctor. Our family will then have both kinds of doctors—your kind and my kind. Last December we missed you in Kolkata and this December Tua and Tia were busy applying to colleges. I wanted to talk to you personally over the phone. It was good to hear from your mother that you feel settled in the US. Sometimes transitions can be difficult. I can tell you it was not easy for me when I moved to Germany. My first time away and that too under the circumstances of our times. If diving into student politics had been difficult, then leaving those ideals behind was equally, if not more, gut-wrenching. At least your generation does not have to go through that dilemma. Yet staying abroad and staying alone can never be easy. Make lots of friends, Ira. They will become your real family.

I write today to share a memory with you in the hope that it may turn out to be of some use. Your mother told me that you are undertaking a project on Kumartuli for your thesis and you are having a hard time finding women artists. I have been outside the country for a very long time and I don't know much about your line of work. So feel free to ignore the information if it is totally irrelevant. Here I write it for your consideration. It was 1970 and some of our brightest seniors and friends were deeply enmeshed in the uprisings and kept us aware of the happenings across the state through meetings held in our very own college grounds. I was merely in the first year of college but I could envision that if youth like us joined hands and rose up in arms, we could bring about the change that we wished to see. Seeing where I was located in my academic career, perhaps it was a 'bad time' but then there is never an 'ideal' time for a revolution. I got embroiled in the movement. Yes, it was violent and bloodthirsty. Yes, it was dangerous. But we couldn't bring the establishment down by simply engaging in dialog, nestled in a cosy arm-chair. To this date I don't regret my involvement as such. However, my father—your grandfather—was a pacifist and we never saw eye to eye about anything. The establishment that I was fighting against included him. I can tell you that I had been swayed enough by the mass hysteria to almost accept the fact that the annihilation of the class enemy could result in smearing my hands with the blood of my own father! This might come across as monstrous to you and it does to me too, now, but there is power in propaganda. Baba had explicitly asked me to leave the house if I were to continue with my political involvement. In this he unwittingly echoed some of the leaders of the movement who also expected us to leave our houses and move into rural hideouts. I recognize now that my father was right from his perspective. I should have left but I did not. My ties with Kumartuli were too strong.

By ties I don't just mean my actual family but also the friends I had. I was the secretary of the club that you can still see from our house. The club today is nothing like what it used to be. The idle boys spending their time playing carrom and cards are a shame for those of us who played pivotal roles there when it functioned as the heart of the community. Several of the regular club members of our times were fighters like me or, at least, sympathizers. Eventually the police raided our club. I was home at the time. A young boy, who worked with the tea seller, used to deliver tea to our club. He came running to inform me about the boys at the club, whom the police were beating and arresting. Those days this was a commonplace occurrence and I had thought that I was prepared for this. But I panicked. Mother was scared. My sisters and your father, who was very young then, started crying. I did not want my family to be harassed because of me. Most of all, the prospect of police torture terrified me. I ran out the back door. The boy also ran out with me. I will never understand why he felt obliged to accompany me given that he was so young and had nothing to do with our activities. We made our way through the narrow alleys toward the river. I knew that running would not save us. I would be shot if the police spotted me running. They would easily pass it off as an instance of a rebel escaping, resisting arrest. It happened so often those days. But I think I would have still kept running, expecting to be shot every second, if the boy had not led me up the stairs of one of the houses. There was no time to consider whose house this was. I might have thought it was his house. I don't remember. Upstairs a middle-aged woman shrieked on seeing us. I was certain that we would be discovered but she calmed down almost instantly. She did not ask who we were and she did not turn us out. Instead she asked us to go inside. It was somebody's bedroom. We must have been there for less than ten minutes but it felt as though we had been hiding behind that almirah for centuries. I wonder why we stood behind the almirah. If the police entered the house we would be found no matter where we were hiding. I kept hearing knocks on the door. First it was in my mind, then, it was for real. I was shocked when the woman went ahead and opened the door. Sheltering us must have been a trap then, I thought. I noticed that her daughter was in the same room as us. She had been there all along looking at us without saying a word. We heard her mother argue with the police downstairs. She reasoned that she and her daughter are alone in the house and under no circumstances can she let the men enter in the absence of her husband. In what seems like the biggest miracle of my life, the police eventually left.

Later I wanted to visit and thank this woman. I asked the boy, who had accompanied me, whether he knew the family. At the tea shop, he introduced me to the lady's son, whom everyone knew by the name of Babua. When I visited their house the woman's husband was also there. I immediately regretted the visit because it was evident that she had not told her husband about what had transpired. He expressly told us that we were reckless and selfish to have put his family in danger. He was equally, if not more, annoyed with his wife, who had protected us, and even Babua, who had brought us to visit. He ordered me to stay away from Babua and ordered Babua to stay away from the tea shop. I learned that they were a family of idol-makers.

Their workshop's location was known to me but I did not see or hear from them for a few years. Then one evening

Babua came to our club. His father was very sick and had to be hospitalized immediately. Some other boys went out to help. Babua's father survived his illness as far as I remember but I also remember people discussing Babua's sister a lot those days. Apparently, she excelled at idol-making. Though the news about the girl's stint at the studio circulated as much as it did because she was having an affair with one of the workers on her father's payroll. The neighbourhood in Kumartuli was closely knit, so such stories did the rounds. When your mother told me that you are looking for female artisans I immediately thought of her. I had always assumed that she must be working there even now but I guess not. In any case her brother still ought to be there. He was my age, or younger. You can ask around for him. I can give you directions to their house. If you exit through the front door of our house and walk left toward the river, you will find a grocery shop. I am fairly sure it is still there. I used to buy you tamarind candies from there when you were young, remember? Take a right from there. Paramesh uncle's house is at the other end of that lane but don't walk all the way to his house. There is a narrow lane toward the left again before you reach Paramesh uncle's. Actually there might be more than one lane on the left over there. Take the one that is more than half way from the grocery shop—closer to Paramesh uncle's house than the shop. The house, if they haven't re-painted it, should be a shade of green. They had a porch. Stairs led up to the rooms. The ground floor used to house some unsold or damaged idols. I wish I could be more precise with the directions. But it is not too far from our house. I once reached there in less than five minutes. So you can imagine. Ask your father to help you find the place. He knows the directions to Paramesh uncle's house.

I was telling your mother on the phone that I am both surprised and pleased with you for pursuing this project. The idol-makers have always been our neighbours. We—your father, I, and your older uncle—all had friends who were related to the idol-making business in some capacity. What you are doing is commendable. It is up to youngsters like you to ensure that the artisan's stories are not forgotten. They are our culture's pride. I know very little about your research. So don't mind my questions. Why don't you broaden your research agenda? Female artists in Kumartuli are rare. At least they were rare when I was in Kolkata. I don't think that the situation has radically altered in the last 40 years. If you exclusively focus on the women, then you will miss out on the important contributions of the men to this great art. Undoubtedly the men from Kumartuli are some of the finest sculptors in our country.

Every five years we import a new idol from Kumartuli for our Durga Pujo in Stuttgart. As you know, I started the pujo for our Bengali community, even though I stay away from religious rituals myself. The festival brings us, the Bengalis from India and Bangladesh, together in this foreign land. People are always stunned to see the exquisite workmanship of the Kumartuli artisans. Even though the artists sell their idols at premium rates to us, the members of our pujo committee have got so accustomed to the special touch of Kumartuli artists that they don't think twice before placing the orders.

Now, tell me, when are you visiting us? You should get a Schengen visa. Your aunt, sisters, and I want to see you. Your mother stated that you take your flights to Kolkata via Abu Dhabi and New Delhi. Next time when you go to India, stop at Stuttgart for your transit. We will pick you up from the airport and show you around. Your sisters will move out for their college in a few months but they will be back for the holidays. Plan something soon. Your mother calls our house in Kolkata 'a retirement house'. Even I tell your aunt that we should move back once our daughters are off to college but then again I have practised medicine all my life in this country. I will not be able to adjust to the lackadaisical work culture of Kolkata. I hope you don't mind that I have given your e-mail address to Tia and Tua. They are interested in going to America for higher studies, just like you. I told them that they are getting ahead of themselves. They have not even begun college. All you sisters are so focused on your careers. What can I say? We are so proud of you all. We look forward to seeing you soon.

Lol, MejKa.

with best regards,
Sumit Chatterjee

P.S: I thought lol stands for lots of love but Tua tells me it means laughter. Either way, be well!

8

Search: *Bhul Bhulaiya*
Wednesday, 17 July 2013
10:30 PM

from: Fasahat Zaidi <zaidi.fasahat@h-mail.com>
to: ira.chatterjee12@h-mail.com; s.rizwan85@h-mail.com

Fasahat: Turns out Rizwan isn't the only revolutionary Ira knows!

Rizwan: My name is Rizwan and I am not a revolutionary.

me: You guys, that's why I know a thing or two about revolutionaries. ;) For all his revolutionary ideals, Mejka turned out to be the most selfish of dad's siblings. My grandfather, with whom he supposedly never saw eye to eye, spent a fortune to send him abroad and soon enough he got married and settled over there. Thanks to him, my grandfather had limited liquid assets left to sponsor my aunts' weddings or my dad's education. I even doubt whether Mejka was all that involved in any transformative activity. If my parents are to be believed, no young guy in Kolkata during the period could remain untouched by the happenings. So, nbd. Besides, don't you find his e-mail's tone all-knowing and condescending?

Fasahat: Dollops of abhiman is the lubricant you need to turn the plot. Stories have holes in them for you to enter and change their course.

me: Whose story are we talking of now?

Rizwan: Trust me, not even Fasahat knows. Haha.

me: How come you guys pinged me together?

Fasahat: I am watching kites claim their bit of the summer sky. An unwinding spool's squeaks are scoring the show. I see the three of us reaching for the thread....

Rizwan: We are in the same room, sitting next to each other, in my apartment in Kalkaji. Also, for the record, I am not a revolutionary, the sky is overcast, n there are no kites here.

me: No way! And here I am; the only high point of my life being weekend bbqs. I wish I had gone to India this summer but I got this teaching assignment :(I was just searching flights for late August, so I could look for the person Mejka mentions before the autumn semester began, but the tickets are so freaking expensive.

Fasahat: Can't you ask the idol-makers' union for her contact details now that you know of her?

me: I will ask them but given my experiences through the last one year, I no longer hold their ledgers in very high esteem. What are you desi boys up to?

Fasahat: Rizwan is too busy for anything. He came back to town last night and is leaving tomorrow. I have to make my way through the *bhul bhulaiya* that is Old Delhi.

Rizwan: I bet u want to know what Fasahat has been up to. I'll tell you. He stares at the different gates in Delhi—Ajmeri gate, Kashmiri Gate...blah blah. He finds his way to these ruins and spends hours by the road waiting for some fleeting vision. This exercise is followed by his frantic search for related historical documents and then he concocts tales that have little to do with the sources he just consulted. At the heart of his poem cycle is a whining girl, who wants to learn to write but can't bring herself to do it for no particular reason.

me: Yeah, that's a good summary of the collection he has been writing :)

Rizwan: What?! u knew n never pointed out the absurdity of it? As in, what is the point he is trying to make?

Fasahat: Poetry doesn't need to have a point.

Rizwan: Everything needs to have some point. Why do u write? Why does anyone write?

me: Not again, Riz. You boys, play it nice in Dilli :) I am off to lesson plan.

Monday, 29 July 2013
10:30 PM

from: Fasahat Zaidi <zaidi.fasahat@h-mail.com>
to: ira.chatterjee12@h-mail.com

Ira, Tausif is not holding up. So I returned to Asharfabad; yet, I can not but wonder when the gates of Delhi will open for me. I never fancied petting parrots, then why do I have to sleep with couplets brawling in my head? Fortunately, Tausif has an old record player to distract me. Maybe I can buy one for myself. A shop, which has sprung up across my house here, buys and sells second-hand electronic items. The teenager running it probably knows nothing of the goods he is trading. It could be that the items he is selling belonged to people I knew.

On some days, I scarcely recognize this place. This is the land where red avadavats flew out of cooked samosas when we uttered bismillah. When one placed murabba in one's mouth it turned into meat. If one was bold enough to bite glass, then the shards turned into granulated sugar. But none of it lingered. You know, for my nani's wedding, her mother had handpicked hundreds of saris. Before her death, Nani watched those saris burn in the open street right outside the threshold she had once crossed as a bride. A flaming torch devoured the ornate muqaish patterns in golden and silver wire. She could not take her eyes off the smoke that rose from the fabric she had wrapped around her petite figure not too long ago. The executor of the rite was absorbed in collecting the molten gold and silver. It was the price she paid for having sons and a husband who were above service of any kind. Hoarding is a privilege that will not endure.

Love and grief, on the other hand, seldom disperse. At about the same time when my Nani observed the rising smoke without blinking her eyes, my Dadi was navigating this *bhul bhulaiya* of a city with tears in her eyes. Once Dadi was a celebrated singer of marsiyas. Dadaji fell in love with her voice. A done-to-death tragedy was enacted thence: at a performance within a year of their wedding, Dadaji spotted Dadi talking to a young man with her eyes. That was the end of her public career as a sozkhwan. It was also the beginning of an indefinite period of mourning. She confined herself to a room in the house, composed marsiyas, and sang to herself. Even before Abbu reached his teens, Dadi took to the habit of drifting across the streets at odd hours. Often she would be found and brought back by some acquaintance. While she never cried within this house, tears rolled down her cheeks the moment she stepped out. Grief killed her soon after. Her notes and compositions have been burnt. Her articles were distributed among needy relatives. Yet her love for music and poetry and her enduring grief never left this house. I know Abbu sees her in me.

Every summer, the loo sweeping this city catches me off guard. A scooter hit a bicyclist right around the corner of the street. Abbu will surely be called to attend to the scene. My laptop is on the brink of exploding. Now I will be heading to the bookstore in the Chowk where Tausif and I met for the first time about eight years ago, following several years of corresponding with each other. That afternoon Tausif was reading aloud bits and pieces from the books while browsing the shelves. You would think it would disturb the others but he was enjoying the sound of the words rolling out of his mouth so much so that it was heartwarming even for the onlooker. Of late I have been thinking whether coming back to India for a few years would be such a bad idea after all. This is more than nostalgia: it's like climbing down a flight of stairs that you know can take you only in one direction. Tausif wants someone to take over *Taqreer*. I could do that and find a teaching position to support myself.

Warmly,
FZ

Friday, 9 August, 2013
7:30 AM

from: Fasahat Zaidi <zaidi.fasahat@h-mail.com>
to: ira.chatterjee12@h-mail.com

Ira, I am writing to you from what was Dadi's room. The room, which has since been occupied by generations of cousins draws me today in a way that no other room of this house does. But when I was growing up, it was not the same. I was continually looking for opportunities to enter the small room on the ground floor: Abbu's chamber. Most of Abbu's patients suffered from dreary ailments such as fevers, headaches, hot flashes, irregular bowel movements. Yet, each of them fetched a distinct story to explain the onset of the disease and its symptoms. If one eavesdropped on the chamber's doors, like I did, one would recognize the creativity of germs and viruses, which could enter one's body in a hundred different ways to ensure the same outcome. The white globules that Abbu handed his patients were the other incentive. I knew, if I stared at the globules long enough, Abbu would offer me a sugary blend of the powders and potions.

Intermittently Abbu's patients brought uncanny tales into our house. I remember one such instance in which a black burqa clad woman storms into Abbu's chamber. It is a common enough sight at first but something about her movement flusters me. As soon as she enters the chamber and shuts the door behind her—a gesture which was optional for Abbu's patients—she begins to wail. The walls of the chamber make abortive attempts at containing her moans. Something is gnawing at her heart. I peep in through the narrow gap between the two flanks of the chamber's door.

Abbu courteously extends a transparent plastic cup filled to the brim with water, even as he is visibly disconcerted. His knit brows with which I was acquainted betrays his desire to get rid of her at the earliest. After a few minutes, the woman slips her palms beneath her veil and wipes her cheeks. She needs help falling asleep. And she lifts the veil to testify to her month-long insomnia. The dense shadows cast around her eyes suggest clotted blood rather than dark circles. As she collects herself and continues to speak, her philtrum creases into a narrow moustache. The toe of her canvas sneakers beat the concrete floor at regular intervals. Abbu refuses to prescribe pills without diagnosing the cause of her ailment. In response, the woman identifies her husband as the source of her consternation. Abbu suggests the usual: she should talk to her husband and reconcile with him rather than take sleeping pills. At this she bursts into tears, again. He, whom she married, no longer exists.

I conclude her husband must have expired but Abbu does not interrupt her. Whether he keeps silent for wanting to hear more or because he is confounded, I can not tell. The woman takes his silence as her cue to elucidate. Grabbing his prescription pad, she starts doodling with quivering hands. I recovered this drawing from the chamber's dustbin much later but let me tell you right away what it was. The diagram comprises concentric circles with myriad passageways connecting them. You can enter the design through a singular opening but once inside the paths ramify and diverge. In case you continue to move in any one direction, you return where you began. The woman runs her ball-point pen anti-clockwise around the innermost circle. Her husband, she explains, is entrapped in that central hole, which is hundreds of feet deep and full of numbing water.

If there is any truth to the woman's account, then it is a matter for the police to resolve. Or, so Abbu reasons. But she does not relent. She is certain that once Abbu hears the entire story he will understand why she has come to him. The woman's husband was a stonemason, who specialized in carving and inscribing headstones and cenotaphs. His mallets and gouges cut iridescent mihrabs in granite, illustrating the parable of Light. His fingers swiveled letters into acts

of supplication. Three to four months ago he joined a team
of craftsmen employed by the government to conserve and
restore the city's historical monuments. In general, our
narrator does not take much of an interest in her husband's
work. After all, why revere robust headstones and dilapidating
shrines? She merely heeds any odd anecdotes he volunteers
every now and then. For example, during an earlier phase
of the restoration project, he was commissioned to shape a
headstone for a prominent poet who had arrived in the city in
the eighteenth century. The poet's tomb was to be recuperated
as a tourist attraction but the crew appointed to place the
headstone could not locate the grave. It didn't matter in the
end because the stonemason got paid anyway.

More recently her husband was hired to restore a three-
century-old labyrinth, a *bhul bhulaiya*, in the heart of the city.
This labyrinth is the subject of her sketch. She explains that
all the concentric circles are not on the same level. The tunnel
leading any entrant is not a path charted on flat surface; rather
it consists of thousands of steep stairs and half a thousand
identical doors. Even during the day, darkness shrouds most of
the passages. The stonemason carries torches, spare batteries,
matches, and lanterns on his way to work. During the sweltering
summer of our city, the structure assumes a particularly stifling
character. As a result, the workers grow more impatient every
day. They hope to complete the restoration urgently. However,
an unusual challenge presents itself: work done on the side
of the central vault through any particular day is reversed
by the next morning. The central vault is also the site of the
hole with water—the well—in the woman's sketch. The
husband frequently laments that the project will never end.
The stonemason's wife is not perturbed since he earns his daily
wages not withstanding the reversible nature of the monument.

One day, while at work, the stonemason spots a woman throwing pebbles into the well. Her shoulders move with the agility of a practised stone-skipper. He imagines her eyes lusting for restless ripples. The shafts of light entering the dark vault from the arched windows bounce off the well's walls. On gathering she is being watched, the woman turns toward the stonemason and invites him to join her. She hands him a few well-rounded stones. No sooner does he join her than he realizes that the stones sink as soon as they touch the surface, without splashing even a drop of water or forming ripples. The water in the well, the woman informs, runs so deep that it will be hours before the stones kiss the ground. But once they do, they shall be renewed.

The legend piques the stonemason's interest. He asks what form the renewed stones take. The woman does not answer. Instead she introduces herself as Ghaddar and remarks that the Gomti is not the source of the well's water. What a masculine name, the stonemason thinks to himself and says as much while recounting the episode to his wife. Next afternoon he finds Ghaddar again, at the same place. While relating the first rendezvous I forgot to mention that the stonemason had not seen Ghaddar's face for it was covered by the burqa. So he recognizes Ghaddar from the anklet she wears. They greet one another and Ghaddar enquires about the status of his work. Her own expeditions to the labyrinth are prompted by her yearning for complete darkness, which is scarce these days. The sight of the well soothes her for in it she sees the possibility of donning a new body, perhaps a customizable one; unscathed and free from the wear and tear of her current frame. The stonemason's wife suspects that her husband must have kept up his meetings with Ghaddar even after those cursory ones and eventually, his exchanges with Ghaddar must have graduated from spiritual to more earthly concerns.

I can see that the stonemason's wife's tale is trying Abbu's patience. If she were a man, Abbu would have asked her to leave. I require her to finish the story before Abbu usurps her from the patient's chair. Luckily, the woman seems completely oblivious of Abbu's disgruntled face. Presently the stonemason starts complaining about the sheer amount of work assigned to him. He tells his wife that it is the work that keeps him in the labyrinth hours after sundown. His wife grows apprehensive. She considers visiting him at work unannounced. However, other household obligations come in the way of executing such a scheme until one night her husband does not return. She waits, sighs, and cries.

The morning following that sleepless night, her in-laws curse her for failing to keep her husband bound to her bed. She rushes to the labyrinth in search of him. On probing she learns that her husband had been at work the previous day. However, this morning he is yet to make an appearance. Reluctantly, she asks whether he had been seen interacting with any visitors to the labyrinth on a regular basis. The masons look at one another and confirm that he often chats with a woman near the well who knows many deep secrets and recites from scriptures. The stonemason's wife walks up to the well in the vault but she neither finds Ghaddar nor her husband.

As she makes her way back from the labyrinth, she grasps that her husband has abandoned her. There is little room for any doubt. But then, he returns! Questions about the previous night might ruffle the feathers. So she selects to forego her anger and grievance. They lie side by side at night. When he turns toward her under the quilt, her hands trace the contours of his body. Her lips are soggy with seeping saliva. The tips of her fingers mount the ridge south of his navel. The rough hair, the streaming sweat, as she has always known them. Yet, her familiarity with the niches of his body end there. Dazed, her fingers retrace their way across the navel to encounter his chest drooping like a pair of ripe pears. The stonemason presses his palm over her gaping mouth.

They set off anew. She glides past the flushed skin of her cleavage, re-orienting herself. As she gently caresses the back of her ear on the way to her nape, she grabs her wayward hand, pins it to a dent on the pillow and tastes her supple tits. The bones of her hip rub against the contracting flesh of her abdomen. With a jolt she frees her arm from her hard grip, flips over, and locks her shoulders. Her quick breath tickles her. She bites the tip of her nose. She feels her body move in circles, its axis being the one leg stuck between the two of hers. Her knuckles make a cracking sound as they weave their fingers. She wraps her knees around her. The refrain of a song she heard on the eve of her wedding melts in her mouth. Once outside their room, the stonemason and her wife conduct their lives in ways that mask their forms. But when left to themselves, they slit the coverings with increasing haste. Ghaddar, the stonemason happily recalls, had facilitated the transformation.

Despite the cautions the couple exercise, the stonemason's brother discovers her naked body. He announces its kinks to whoever he meets until one day people drag the stonemason to the Chowk, tie her up, and strip her to see for themselves. They pull her wife by her hair and fastens her hands to a rod. When the stonemason closes her eyes, she is haunted by the sight of her wife's and her charring bodies. She starts pleading with those who hold them hostage. Given a day's time, she asserts, she could remedy the situation by turning herself into who she used to be. She is allowed to return to the labyrinth half in jest, as the crowd prepares itself for delayed gratification. Her wife spends the night stretched on the stairs of the labyrinth. She gropes the musty air to feel the engraved names of generations of lovers on its wall. The stonemason re-appears the next morning and walks up to the Chowk, stark naked. The crowd is fascinated by the karamat but also, disappointed. They abandon the couple. However, the stonemason and his wife can not disremember the person he had become. None of them get any sleep. The stonemason spends his nights at the labyrinth. He has discovered that the only restoration work that endures in the central vault is that which is completed at night. His wife lies on her bed with eyes shut, without getting any sleep.

Abbu is most relieved as the narrative comes to a screeching halt. His eyes are directed toward the floor and patches of sweat have stained his shirt. He hastily rips the topmost page of his writing pad where the woman had doodled, throws it into the dustbin, and scribbles a prescription. This is followed by his usual gig of blending powders. The woman leaves his chamber armed with a pouch of cloying globules.

Abbu always refuses to acknowledge the occurrence of this incident. He says he never saw such a patient and claims that I made it all up even though I have vivid memories of the episode. To tell you the truth, I only merely contrived the story's conclusion. The stonemason's wife's tale had ended with a shriek resulting from the encounter with her husband's new body. Keeping it a secret from others was preventing her from getting sleep. But if I let the story end there, you would dismiss it claiming that a certain Mr Freud explained the event even before it transpired. Hence, the liberties I took.

The essential thing about this story, or any story, is not how it ends but what becomes possible while it lasts.

Love,
FZ.

9:30 AM

from: ira.chatterjee12@h-mail.com
to: zaidi.fasahat@h-mail.com

Oi, Zaidi! I can hardly believe I wasted the first half hour of my morning reading this story. Don't try to pull a fast one on me. Just because I have never been to your city doesn't mean I know nothing of it! Mom grew up there and I read that book you lent me, remember? You have repurposed myths about THE *Bhul Bhulaiya*, duh! Your e-mails communicate nothing of substance these days. Only obscure fabrications of different sorts and then, there were no grandmas, chefs, poets, or Nawabs to salvage this one. Anyways, when's your flight landing on Sunday? Amber can come pick you up from the airport but I haven't yet shifted the kitchenware from my previous apartment. So, just a heads up, you might want to eat at the airport or we can get some takeaway. Btw, I did manage to track the female idol-maker, Pratima Paul, and spoke to her on the phone yesterday. I will meet Dr Harris later today and inform her of the same. She'll be relieved I suppose. It is a pity though that I couldn't make it to Kolkata this summer. So the interview has to wait until December but, at least, now it will happen. Phew!

9

Interviewer: Ira Chatterjee
Location: Kumartuli, Kolkata
Transcriber and Translator: Ira Chatterjee

The interviewees were debriefed about the project and were handed a set of prompts on the spot. S/he then spoke freely without the interviewer intervening apart from reassuring remarks or monosyllabic responses such as 'yes', 'certainly', 'right'. Unless otherwise indicated, the interviewees narrated in Bengali. (-) marks incomplete sentences. [unclear] denotes speech that could not be deciphered.

Thursday, 19 December 2013
Interviewee #15: Pratima Sarkar (nee Paul)

My name is Pratima Paul. It is my daughter who is interviewed more often. So, she knows what to say, unlike me. I started the whole thing—my work—in order to give her a hand. The kind of idol-making that you are asking about, yes, I did it at one time, you are right. But that was only once—one year—a long time ago. I learned from following the men who worked at Baba's workshop. When I was a child, Baba taught me to mould clay dolls. I understood his work. Growing up in Kumartuli, if you are attentive, you learn. But, I did not receive any formal training. When I started working, I would observe others and emulate what they were doing. I can not explain how, what happened.

I carved the idols with a lot of fervour and then, to be honest, when I got married (-). My in-laws' family was huge. My sisters-in-law, my brothers-in-law—looking after them, getting them married at a proper age into the right families. All these responsibilities, I had to fulfil. Then these [unclear] consuming certainly. What more to say? Now these are not today's incidents. You are asking about events that occurred 30–40 years ago. I [unclear], after that what did I do? Did nothing. My in-laws were business people. They had a shop of sweets on Ramdulal Street, founded in 1876. Very famous sweet shop. These days children don't like sweets, so you may not know. I had had sweets from that shop even as a girl. Before I knew (-). They cast sweets into a variety of shapes.

The year I got married, everyone knew about my work in Kumartuli. My father-in-law encouraged me to join the sweets shop when I was a newlywed. So I moulded a pratima's [idol's] face the first year. But after that I did not keep up my involvement in their business. Was there a dearth of things to do? Where was the time to mould and craft sweets? Besides, business is something I have never grasped. That's why I did not have anything to do with my father's workshop either. My brothers-in-law and their sons work with my husband. I never had the time to join them on top of everything else I did as the family's eldest daughter-in-law. Are you married, yet? My daughter has to ensure her husband carries lunch to his office before she leaves for her studio.

I [unclear]. What I had to do? Cook, serve food, keep the house in order, work for everyone else, the usual. We had maids but the women in the house were the ones responsible for the smooth running of the household. Besides, within a year of my wedding my elder daughter was born. After that I couldn't even find the time to come to Kumartuli. As long as Baba was alive, Ma had company. Whenever I came, I saw the idol-making continue as usual. If you ask the artists here you will learn that the idol-making business has been on the verge of extinction for a long time. We would think of every year as the last year because of the rate at which expenses increased. But in the end, the work would still go on.

You were asking if I learned from anyone. Now I remember someone in particular, besides Baba, of course. The year I joined Baba's workshop, I was still quite uncertain about the processes. So, at the outset, I was happy with whatever little I could do. Baba would not even want me to touch the idols, if he were around. So, being able to enter the workshop without restrictions, while he was recovering, was a significant achievement. There were one or two people who guided me at the time. The person I specifically recall was different from all the other artisans. He would not chit-chat but I could make out that he looked at me with affection. I reminded him of his daughter, who was my age and was suffering from tuberculosis that season. What a kind man he was! You know, there was something that I did not understand then. Now that I look back to those times, I get a sense of it but I am baffled at how it was even possible. This man was working on Durga idols but I think he was Muslim. I had seen him pray. It was in the Muslim way. I had accidentally walked into a corner we had at the back of the shop. But I am not sure. How had nobody else noticed? You see, that explains why he fasted till sundown. No, I never saw him after I left the workshop following Baba's return.

Other than this, what more? Other stories from the [unclear]. Baba managed the family business till the last day of his life. He was competent and loved sculpting idols. Then my brother took over but he failed to sustain it. When our workshop's fortune was fast declining, I asked my husband whether we should do something about it, if I should help out. But what my husband said was correct—we don't understand or know the business. I myself perhaps appreciate the idol-making practices but I don't get the financial side. So, by intervening, we would damage the prospects further, my husband said. And he was, of course, right. My brother died of stomach infection almost 10 years ago. His wife was from Shantipur and she returned there immediately, leaving Ma alone.

If Baba were alive to see what my daughter is doing, he would be pleased. She does excellent work. I was not that good, you know. So Baba did not want me to meddle with the idols that everyone worships. Sculpting idols is no child's play. I did not realize it at the time. I was in school but all I wanted to do was work in Baba's workshop, like my brother. To be honest with you, I was not interested in studies. Our [unclear] was terrible. And I did not have much use for reading and writing. I had no idea that one can eventually study about idol-making or sculpting. Others my age from Kumartuli perhaps knew better. Quite a few boys I grew up with went to colleges where famous national and international artists teach sculpting. Only recently I have learned of the possibilities that were there.

When my daughters started attending school—I have two daughters—I would not be able to help them too much with their lessons. But I admitted them in an English-medium school. Because I knew if they wanted to accomplish anything in their lives, they would need to read and write English. Their father, at first, was very hesitant. How will they turn out if they go to an English-medium school? That was his chief concern. Neither of us, he or me, went to an English school. If they study there—you know, how people think differently over there—he was rightly worried about that. However, I stressed that if they have to study, let them study in English school. We will see. If we can not carry on, then we will admit them elsewhere. Let them start, at least. So then, after that, my daughters studied. Both my daughters turned out to be bright students. I never had to wear out the sole of my sandal to keep track of them or their studies. They accomplished everything on their own.

Baba was never as well-off as my husband. And about fifteen years ago, my husband's family opened new branches of their shop in other parts of Kolkata. It further boosted the sales. My husband now worries that neither of his children will join the flourishing family business. But, he and I agree that our daughters should do what they want. And that's what I keep explaining to everyone else as well.

My elder daughter, as you found out, is a sculptor. The younger one was good at sketching but she studied Maths and is currently preparing for Banking entrance exams. She will work in proper offices. When my elder daughter was growing up, she would remind me of my girlhood. She enjoyed drawing and playing with clay, just like me. Like me, she would win prizes for her sketches, here and there. Nobody trained me but I supported her as much as I could. After completing an entire day's housework I would take her to drawing classes in the evening. I would see to it that she took time out at home to complete her sketches. For her tenth birthday, my husband and I got her a mouldable plastic kit. We put in similar efforts for both my daughters. The younger one fared better in her studies. Though she was even more intelligent than my elder daughter, she was not all that interested in the world beyond her books.

The elder [unclear]. When she finished school, she announced that she wanted to study art. Very well, I thought. I was initially considering, perhaps [unclear]. By then, Baba's business was in a bad shape. Still I thought my elder daughter can join the workshop and make idols, eventually. However, she was interested in other sorts of sculptures. She can look at people's photos and replicate them with close precision. You give someone's photo to her—give her your photo—she will make a statue that looks exactly like you, including the alternating black and red strands of hair.

I received an unexpected reward when my daughter started her own studio. I told her I like to see her work and would visit the studio often. At home now everyone is grown up. My mother-in-law and father-in-law are no more. So I have time on my hands. Long back, I had confided in my daughter that at a younger age, I desired to make idols—the entire story about how I would go to my father's shop when my father was in the hospital and so on. She was fairly young when I first told her that story. Don't know if she recalled it at all or not. Later when I told her again, she asked, Ma do you want to sculpt? Do you want to carve any models? Now I [unclear]. They are so well-educated. They have formally studied this. In her studio, me? I would break something perhaps, what would I do? I told her, no, no, I don't want to get in the way. She invests in the materials. I can not spoil things bought with her hard-earned money. But she pressed me, saying, Ma if you want to learn, I can teach you. At the time, I thought I am no longer at the age when I can learn. Yet, she can be very stubborn sometimes. She stressed, Ma, see you can do it, you can do it, you have to do it.

If she had not insisted as much, I would never revive what I thought was permanently gone. When I was at the age to pursue this craft, it was different. That era is behind us. But she—she held my hands—you understand, right? This is so [unclear]. What shall I say? That forgotten aspiration I had—the desire that the young girl had—that desire no one [unclear; pause]. No one had considered it at the time. No one wanted to know what I wanted. They got me married. Actually I wanted to get married. But when I held the chisel to work with my daughter, how to put it in words? Those days were here again. I was not sure if I would be able to accomplish anything. I would wonder, why is she getting me into all this? I will be able to do nothing. I will be in her way. The faith my daughter had in me—no one else had shown that kind of conviction previously. She held my hands, she held my hands! What was her need? She was highly skilled. She had studied and was receiving prestigious assignments.

One of her first assignments was to carve statues of different scientists for a college in Kharagpur. They had sent her the photos. Gradually my daughter also employed other people to collaborate with her. Her hands were full but amid all that—no, no Ma, you do it; if you want you can do it. What she has given me, I can not describe. And no one can understand. So after that I learned. I gradually learned to work. It has been 8 to 9 years now. I would work with her, on her assignments. Nothing on my own. But then—how many years ago was it? Must be 5–6 years?—she received this order. You have seen those sculptures at the crossroads of busy streets, right? She was commissioned to make a model like that. They told her [unclear]. In general she would be asked to carve particular models resembling famous people. Like Gandhiji, Netaji, Shivaji. For this assignment, they said she could make anything she wanted.

So my daughter said, Ma if you want, you can take this one. I was baffled—what will I make? What do I know? All I could carve on my own was the Durga idol. I can sculpt idols like that. So then I told her we could create a swan or a Durga pratima. That's how I was thinking. However, she asked me to resist thinking that way: why don't you think in a different way? She said, the model does not have to be an idol, does not have to be like anyone else, anything else. It could be something entirely new. She then showed me photos of numerous sculptures from far and wide, from our country and the rest of the world. Lots of talented people had crafted those models. Models that you can look at for hours but not make out precisely what they are. Even though they don't take the form of any known object, they engage the viewer. I tried to conceive of something along those lines. She told me that I was free to craft as I chose. I began drafting—first, on paper. For me, to be honest, it was too challenging to forgo the style to which I was accustomed from the moment I had opened my eyes. It is easy to say that we don't need to make a model that looks like anything else but if a model is like nothing else, then what is it like?

So I told my daughter, we could follow some designs—like what we do for *alpona* but my daughter said, don't do that. The flowers, leaves, paisleys—move past those. Flowers and leaves are like flowers and leaves. So then what do I make? I kept trying and my daughter continued to reject my drafts. Finally what I made you can see. A 25-feet sculpture. It stands at the intersection of Belaghata and bypass. Yes, it is still there, of course. That is my first solo work. As in, solo meaning, you see my daughter was still the lead artist. The assignment had come to her. But the concept we finally executed was mine. It was prompted by her, obviously, as she wouldn't let me sculpt flowers, leaves, or idols. What I crafted in the end, it is there for you to see.

These days I regularly go to my daughter's studio. Most assignments we get are for statues because my daughter's speciality is that. I handle some small assignments on my own from time to time but I have totally parted ways with idol-making. If I want I can sculpt some plaster or fiberglass idols but, you can say that it no longer excites me. Baba's workshop is no more, as I told you. I had grown up seeing him work there and now I am happy to join my daughter. I do not have it in me or even desire to do something separately, on my own. Whatever my daughter says I will do that. I held the chisel again because of her. And when I did, my husband—well, he never says yes or no to anything, ever. When I started working with my daughter, he did not object. What is it to him? If food and house are in order, then he can hold nothing against me. After all, it is with our daughter that I work, not with some third person. So he never said no. In fact, I can not say that he has ever objected to me working, to be honest. Even when I came as a newlywed, it is not as if anyone said no, you should not make idols. At the same time, no one told me that I could go ahead and spend my days at Baba's workshop. It was the year before I got married that the incident had happened—I had been at the workshop in Baba's absence and people discussed it. Baba finally caught me red-handed at work. No family member had disclosed anything to him when he was at the hospital and convalescing at home but he was suspicious of what I was going about doing. I would work during the school hours, you see. When Baba found out, he was so annoyed. He gave me a nice thrashing. I said, *na*, I did not harm your shop, please let me continue. Baba said, I asked you to study. From his side he was right. He wanted me to study. For getting married also one needs to study. And I had really neglected my school work. So Baba kept lamenting, you don't go to school and waste time doing what you are not supposed to do! Is it the time for you to do all this? Anyhow, when I got married, I myself admitted to my husband that I had worked in Baba's shop, without his knowledge, the previous year. Because, what's the use—if he gets to know later—then he may be angry with me. My husband carefully listened to me. Up to that. We never discussed the episode afterward.

If you want to know more about the actual work, talk to my daughter. She is the real artist. Which material is what, and what differences exist in the available materials and styles for sculpting, what has changed over the years—she can tell you everything. You know, when my daughter needed space for her initial assignments, my brother did not agree to have her in the family workshop. Apparently, he needed all of the floor space for his dwindling idol-making projects. Finally, however, my brother had to sell the space to repay his debts. A public urinal has come up at the location where we used to have our workshop. What's more, my brother did not leave a penny for his own wife and his children. That's why his wife left for Shantipur to move in with her parents. She realized that there's nothing in Kumartuli for her. I could not, of course, borrow money from my husband to help my brother's family out. And given that I did not work, I had no means of my own. Ma would somehow survive on whatever my brother got from selling what we had. Meanwhile, my daughter stood on her own feet. Now my daughter and I support my mother and my brother's children. Again it is my daughter—she says Ma, if you want to help out your mother, then do it. So I do it. Am I rambling now? You don't want these stories, right? But other than this what more can I say?

I don't come to Kumartuli that often any more. There was a time when this was everything, now what is left of it? Old, yes, old acquaintances are there. I used to know your aunt, Shona Chatterjee. Everyone knew her. Fair, like a *memsahib*, no? Who lives in your house these days? As long as my mother is here I will continue to visit like I did today. But I don't know what will happen after that. Today only, see, a long-time neighbor—Bhola, you know him? He was somewhat unique, could not talk—passed away in an accident. I know the family. I will call on them in the evening before returning to the studio.

You interview my daughter. She will explain in depth how things are done, what we do. The first model I made is there at the intersection of Belaghata and bypass. I can give you the exact address. You can go see it. You can take its photo. We clicked this photo when it was in the studio, still under construction. You see this part? The hole in the middle was something I thought would be good but my daughter did not agree at first. She asked, what is that for? To lead Sita to the earth's womb? Or tempt crows to dive into a well with no water? I told her, the hole is nothing and not anything else. Then she agreed. I never used the brush you see in my hand in the picture for the actual sculpture. I did not know what do to with my hands while posing, so I grabbed that brush from my daughter's desk. She took the photo. You can get the negative from her. Do you want to know anything more? You can come with me to our studio and learn of the orders we are fulfilling at present. If you want to see anything, you are most welcome but the only thing is that we don't make idols there.

Some women perhaps make idols—you may find them. Instead of going by word of mouth, you can simply walk from workshop to workshop in the Kumartuli lanes. Maybe you will find more women. But if you want, my daughter can introduce you to her women artist friends. They don't make idols. They paint. They contribute to fine arts exhibitions. People get to see their work in the fine arts academy. Many of them are sculptors like my daughter whereas some others pursue different kinds of commercial art. The guy my daughter married also studied in her college. He is in advertising. Have you seen that tea advertisement on the billboard near Rajballapara? He designed that. The children these days undertake such a variety of creative assignments. They surprise me. Some of my daughter's friends make sets for films. One of them took me to the studio in Tollygunje and I met Prasenjit! So there's a rich range of projects to choose from nowadays. Idol-making has been dynastic and that is its problem. Not many independent artists get into it straightaway. And why will anyone want to get into this anyway? There's not much money to be made and artists have to eat. Sometimes, among my daughter's friends, I meet artists who make idols out of materials such as ivory or sandalwood. But what you see in Kumartuli—shops full of clay, people making huge idols in dingy rooms—that is not to be found anywhere else. Even my daughter agrees.

10

Ctrl+ F: *Fasahat*
Friday, 17 January 2014
3:00 PM

from: Amber Perez <amberscrawls@h-mail.com>
to: ira.chattrejee12@h-mail.com

Hey babe!
How cold is the la-la-land? Don't slip on black ice, miss, while clicking selfies with the snow. I am stoked to be out of the clutches of the Midwestern winters, though Clara misses building snowpersons with Xian and you. Graduation, no snow, and a job as a barista in a coffee shop from where I can even catch glimpses of Clara, makes this a winter for the books. Every morning when I wake up and find Clara next to me, I am grateful and then, terrified, omg this could've been snatched from me. The fam wasn't amused when I conceived her and then, they thought I'm cray to study art in school with a young daughter to look after but if not for my folks, last summer, I would neither have got through Clara's surgery nor would that doctor have let me bring my baby back with me. Those who have fams that look perfect on forms believe that

is how it should be. Clara's doc is a case in point. Prolly she drops her children to daycare and her husband picks them up after work. Baby Jesus be thanked that the doc listened to my parents when they promised to take on Clara's responsibility and agreed to let the matter go. To let Clara go with momma and pop was admitting defeat, momentarily, but it coulda been hell lotta worse. And woot, I'm with my Clara now.

Anyway did you see this viral list, 12 Things Indian Women Do Not Want to Hear, doing the rounds of FB? :). You have to take me and Clara to India. *Fasahat* will show us around his cities and you will show us around yours. We'll have most of the country covered or no? lol…joking. I got to find a real job soon. I love making birds and ferns on people's lattes but it ain't getting me very far. After that med textbook I illustrated, I was kinda hoping to see more of such assignments. Tbh, I didn't follow up or actively seek opportunities, was so caught up in trying to graduate and returning to Anaheim asap. Come Tuesday I have an interview for a 3-year contractual position at a small art school. The pay will barely get Clara and me through the month if I rent my own place. California's wayyyy more expensive than the Midwest, babe. But it'll be better than what I am making at the coffee shop.

In other news, *Fasahat* wrote to me a couple days back asking me to illustrate the cover of an Urdu mag. He's definitely super committed to the language and the Urdu society he's formed. More power to him but who's running it after he's done with the residency this June? Know what Ira, I have been mulling over some other things to do with you two. The past 6 months, you have been living with Zaidi. Have you pondered the lot of your lovefest once he leaves the la-la-land? You needn't explain to me as long as you both know what to expect from each other. In any case, Clara and I are hyped you found the artists you were looking for and passed your comprehensives with flying colors. We look forward to reading your thesis, babe :).

Saturday, 18 January 2014
11:00 AM

from: ira.chattrejee12@h-mail.com
to: amberscrawls@h-mail.com

Amby, Stop calling me out for my infatuation with snow :P. Where I come from, we had to go to hill stations in winter to catch a glimpse of it and once, during a family trip, Mom asked to stop the car we were in next to a rather steep gorge in order to click one photograph with the falling flakes. It's like when people stop cars and click cattle here. Btw…you seem to be having a much better time than *Fasahat* and me. Whoever wants to live with a poet whose primary goal in life is to not be deported once his residency is over?! Last year, about this time, we had the Super Bowl viewing party at Xian's. Clara wouldn't go off to sleep and you wouldn't booze until she did lol. And now, Xian is mostly out of town. Mike has joined a company on the East coast and taken Eliot along with him. So, Zaidi and I are like the old couple that has unwittingly outlived all their friends.

At Café Locale now, Z's actually sitting right opposite me, hammering the keyboard to spit out applications. At least, he's in purple skinny pants and is flaunting a new rose-gold nose stud. I am polishing off cups of macchiato, staring at the computer screen, and looking out of the window for inspiration, which doesn't seem to be in any hurry to come by (yes, I've switched to coffee again. I need all the caffeine, babe, now that I'm writing 24/7. Okay, that's an exaggeration—I'm writing 6 hours a day though. Z hasn't switched to coffee 'cos that'll be the end of the world as we know it). And we're eating lots and lots of bagels. Z has the pathan's metabolism but I'll need someone like Daniel Castellano (read: Chris Messina :)) for a personal trainer to keep me in shape. You remember how there were two rooms on either side of the glass partition at Locale? Now they have only the one room. The other was sold off earlier this month. What's more, you were right about Rustoroma. They aren't re-opening. So much for local, hipster coffee shops.

I was meaning to ask, when will you send me the sketch you promised. See, you should repay your model, especially one who drops her clothes for you. And, the illustration Zaidi commissioned must be for *Taqreer*, a journal his friend runs in India, and not anything do with the Urdu society as far as I can tell. Your concern about the society is legit, of course, and I don't think this society will function once Zaidi leaves. We had no meeting this month 'cos he's occupied with editing his manuscript and writing applications. I tried learning the alphabet from him but it's been a busy year. Besides, our joint study sessions digress into inane conversations.

Tell Clara that she'll have to wait forever to read my thesis. I am merely on my first chapter. Trying to somehow synthesize all the information about women's presence and absence in Kumartuli. The meeting with Pratima and her daughter last month, though, gave me the leads for my second chapter, where I will discuss untrained female sculptors. I'm definitely most psyched to start writing the final chapter, exclusively focusing on Pratima. Isn't it fascinating that this woman's creation is so markedly visible in a busy public space while she straddles discrete art circles, aesthetic traditions, and economies engendered, on the one hand, by the traditional world of Kumartuli and, on the other hand, by the world of the art colleges? She belongs to neither of these in a sense, exists in liminal spaces, but profoundly impacts both. And just, in general, Pratima's amazing. Whenever you go to Kolkata, you have to meet her! Every time I ask her a question, she starts by saying she doesn't know the answer. Then she'll catalog people who could have answered those questions better than her. But finally when she will respond, very tentatively, it will blow your mind. I am in love with this woman.

Tuesday, 11 February 2014
10:13 PM

from: Lavanya Chatterjee <Chatterjee.lavanya@h-mail.com>
to: ira.chatterjee@h-mail.com

dear ira,
please send *fasahat*'s india address to us. for how long he is here? i think of asking someone from your father's delhi office to drop off the package. but, even otherwise it is no problem. these days' courier services are not too bad and they give us a tracking number if we pay for it. we will parcel the clothes you left behind. makes no sense to keep things you can wear now lying around in the house until you visit again in december. please also tell us where you left the manual to the coffee machine. its operation is unnecessarily complex. i tell you we are much better off with nescafe. take care.

Ma

10:25 PM

from: ira.chatterjee12@h-mail.com
to: Lavanya.Chattrejee@h-mail.com

Mom, don't bother about the clothes now. I can do without
a few t-shirts for a year. Besides, I have no idea how long
Fasahat will be in India. He took the first flight he could after
hearing of Tausif. We didn't get to discuss anything then and
he hasn't been in touch since. I suppose it all depends on how
Tausif fares. I hope he recovers fast. It'll be a huge blow to
Zaidi if he doesn't pull through :(.

from: Lavanya Chatterjee <Chatterjee.lavanya@h-mail.com>
to: ira.chatterjee@h-mail.com

Lavanya: you're online?
me: yes, yes. Bolo.
Lavanya: tausif and *fasahat* were childhood friends or what?
me: No, I don't think so. And now please don't ask me if
Tausif's gay.
Lavanya: uff, no. what i have to do with tausif? but ira, don't
be mad at me, ok? maybe, no new guys approach you because
you live with *fasahat*. people are warded off as they mistake
you for a couple. you see what i mean?
me: From when did you turn into one of those marriage-
obsessed moms?
Lavanya: we bengalis are not marriage obsessed. very very
liberal we are.
me: I can see that.

Lavanya: it is a problem with you. you take everything the wrong way.

me: Okay, mom, I'll spill some beans that I thought could wait. I am not the marriage-types. I am happy with domestic partnerships like what I have with Zaidi.

Lavanya: you mean to live with roommates?

me: Not some random roommate. I want to live with someone I am attracted to, as a roommate, yes.

Lavanya: it is a live-in relationship then.

me: Kind of but we don't necessarily need to be sexual partners.

Lavanya: what? i know living with these gay people will be source of trouble one day. now you want to live with men who like other men.

me: Mom, you are not getting it.

Lavanya: i have no need to get it. you need to grow past this habit of tagging along with other people's lovers. it sounds like the bitter truth i know but what can i do? you need psychological therapy.

me: See, that's why I don't like to discuss these things with you. Don't pathologize my preferences. And I am an adult and I can be in any sort of consensual relationship. Only Zaidi gets me.

5 minutes

?????

You there, Mom?

10 minutes

I'm calling, where's your ph?

Why aren't you picking up?

At least talk to me.

Why are you complicating this?

Wednesday, 12 February 2014
2:10 PM

from: Amber Perez <amberscrawls@h-mail.com>
to: ira.chattrejee12@h-mail.com

Hey babe!
There's some news! So, this past October, Xian forwarded me
a call for a grant from prospective women entrepreneurs. She
wanted us to collab for it. It looked super competitive and
I didn't think we had a shot. Xian made a fierce you-know-
nothing-Jon-Snow face at me and handled most of the app
herself. I chimed in with what I could. We basically proposed
to start a small press and exclusively publish therapeutic
writing and art. We sent some samples of the kind of work
both of us had completed in grad school. Guess what? We
got the moneys :) :) :) Ton of work needs to be done but I am
so so stoked about this. Wish *Fasahat* and you were around
to celebrate with us. <3

Thursday, 13 February 2014
9:19 PM

From: Rizwan Syed <s.rizwan85@h-mail.com>
To: ira.chatterjee@h-mail.com

Ira, what's up? ur mother called me last night. What did u
tell her? She's terribly upset with u n me. She was saying
that *Fasahat* n I have turned u nuts. ur mother is under the
impression that u don't want to get married because u want to
cling on to *Fasahat*, who is in love with me. I tried to assure

her that there's no triangle going on here but she wouldn't take my word for it. Just talk to her, ok? years ago when my parents threw me out, I should have tried to reason a little more. My only regret is that I gave up on them without trying hard enough. Of late, I think of calling or visiting them. Perhaps they will come around n if they don't, I'll know it isn't for lack of trying.

Saturday, 15 February 2014
7:02 AM

from: ira.chatterjee@h-mail.com
to: Rizwan Rizwan <s.rizwan85@h-mail.com>

me: Oi, Riz!

Rizwan: It must be early morning there, right? Up so early?

me: Yeah. Achcha, Riz, did Zaidi get in touch with you?

Rizwan: About what?

me: Generally. He's in India. Did he tell you about Tausif?

Rizwan: Why? What happened?

me: Last week Zaidi learned that Tausif has stopped responding to dialysis. He is losing the ability to recognize familiar faces and hardly eats. After getting that call from Tausif's cousin, Zaidi literally hopped on to a flight. Obviously it was an urgent matter and I informed his department about the sudden turn of events. Anyhow, I had categorically asked Zaidi to keep me in the loop about Tausif's health but I am yet to hear from him.

Rizwan: Well, seeing Tausif this way wouldn't have been easy for *Fasahat*.

me: Of course, I know that. But still. I am anxious. Anyways, do you have Tausif's contacts?

Rizwan: No.

me: But you have friends in the city, right? Meenal?

Rizwan: Kind of. What do you want them to do?

me: Ask Meenal to check on *Fasahat* and Tausif.

Rizwan: So, Ira, Meenal was never in Asharfabad. She works for KARM in Delhi. Both *Fasahat* n I knew her through the organizing work we did, so her name sprang to my mind as a convenient alias. The friend in Asharfabad that u asked me about was Fatima Ali. I did not—

me: WHAT????

2 minutes

Rizwan: Yes, you were obsessing about Fatima at the time and I did not want to bring up things

And I'm no longer in touch with Fatima, so

me: WHAT THE FUCK

What things? I knew there was something about Fatima Ali. *Fasahat's* denial about knowing her work was enough for me to guess as much.

Rizwan: But it has nothing to do with *Fasahat*. That's the thing. n I have lost touch with Fatima since. So, there's nothing more to it.

me: How do I trust you now? I wish I could go there and see what's going on for myself. *Fasahat* and Fatima have to be related. I'm certain now.

Rizwan: Ira…Ira…don't get hysterical. ur mother already suspects u r going mad. relax, u will get ur Zaidi back :-)

me: I don't think I'm getting my Mom back any time soon. Let alone Zaidi.

Rizwan: u haven't talked to her yet?

me: I was silly to broach the topic on chat. She's not taking my calls and refuses to let Dad speak to me. In her fantasy, I'm the fag hag who will see the light some day.

Thursday, 20 February 2014
11:45 PM

From: ira.chatterjee12@h-mail.com
To: s.rizwan85@h-mail.com

Riz :(*Fasahat* has not yet got in touch with me. While he is erratic with e-mails and communication from time to time, this is definitely a new low. I get it that he must be busy with Tausif but can't he send a short text saying that he has reached and how Tausif is doing? I know you have your plate full, so I feel bad for badgering you about this but can you just go down yourself to find out what's up with Zaidi? His mails have stacked up in the house and while most are spams, advertising free pizza and credit cards, some might actually be from the places he's been applying for teaching jobs and residencies. And you owe me a favor for having lied about Fatima. Hell! you still owe me an explanation for it.

from: Rizwan Rizwan <s.rizwan85@h-mail.com>
to: ira.chatterjee@h-mail.com

Rizwan: Ira, what have u been up to beyond checking ur inbox for *Fasahat*'s emails and driving everyone nuts?

me: The first chapter of my dissertation has turned out to be quite long. So I get to split it. I have two chapters now. That's a win, I guess.

Rizwan: Excellent. How many chapters does a dissertation have?

me: Depends. I think 3 chapters + Intro + Conclusion is the minimum. And there's no maximum.

Rizwan: That's a lot of writing. I am graeful to have opted out of academia.

me: lol. *grateful
You wrote very long answers while in college :P KP once asked how you managed to fill 3 booklets in a one-hour class test!

Rizwan: That was different. I have large and loopy handwriting. Besides, those exams had questions. There were more or less right answers to those questions.

me: A dissertation is also an answer to a question that you ask yourself.

Rizwan: So have u wrapped up whatever interviews u were to record?

me: Mostly. My meeting with Pratima Paul and her daughter was such a success.

Rizwan: Are they supportive of your project? Sometimes artists don't like talking about their work.

me: Oh gosh, Riz. I can't tell you how accommodating they've been
When I got back here and started writing, I had new questions. They agreed to talk to me over the phone and I even skyped with her daughter. When I was interviewing Pratima Paul in Kumartuli, I had this moment of fail :P. She was recounting how her daughter had held her hand and

brought her back to the world of sculpting with tears in her eyes. I also started crying! Even in my recordings, I can hear myself sniffling.

Rizwan: u were the only one in the theater sniffling throughout *Kabhi Alvida Na Kehna*. This is much more dignified.

me: I'm empathic, dude, unlike you.

Rizwan: By the way, Ira, I am in Dhaka and so the *Fasahat*-finding assignment has to wait.

me: Really? When did you go?

Rizwan: Early Saturday morning. I was chatting with u from here even the last time. Had I come a week later, I could catch India vs Bangladesh at the Fatulla stadium, if I could afford it. I've never seen India play on a foreign pitch in person.

me: Local spectators wouldn't take too kindly to your rooting for Dhoni.

Rizwan: Dhoni is injured and out of the Asia cup. Kohli will step in as captain.

me: Okay, I don't follow cricket here. Nobody does :P . What are you doing in B'desh this time?

Rizwan: There are non-profits in Bangladesh whose work overlap with KARM's. We r trying to consolidate our connections with them, providing support n volunteers as n when we can. Also, we're working toward organizing a South Asia-wide conference on LGBTQ health issues during December this year. The event will be hosted in Kolkata n faculty from our college have agreed to participate.

me: Neat.

Rizwan: I'm satisfied with the delegates we have roped in so far. There will be speakers from all walks of life: social workers, activists, artists, scientists. It will truly be interdisciplinary in its scope. If u come down to Kolkata in December, try to attend.

me: Is Fatima Ali speaking at your conference?

Rizwan: that's why I didn't mention her in the first place. No, Ira, no. I had known her for a while years back but she left the scene afterward. No one knows about her. Really.

me: Sure. And has her house in Asharfabad where you ate biryani and what not also vanished?

Rizwan: There are some places to which one can never go back.

me: Gawd, that sounded so Zaidi.

Rizwan: Don't u ever get tired of obsessing about *Fasahat*?

me: Don't you ever get assignments to the US?

Rizwan: Now where did that come from?

But, no. We are more or less focused on South Asia at the moment.

me: You should come here. You know, if you came to the US you could even get married legally. At least, in some states. :)

Rizwan: And what good would that do?

me: Riz, some things are better here.

Rizwan: Ha! Like what? What if my gaysian Muslim body spends friendless evenings among the upwardly mobile white faggots in some cruising spot of the Castro? What if my bleeding, starving self, folded in white sheets, rummages dreams, memories, stories to stay afloat?

me: Zaidi visited Castro. He even wrote to me from there. He had a good time.

Rizwan: Do u write or act in street plays anymore?

me: No. Lots of those happen here, of course. Plays to protest racism, against marginalization of the LGBTQ, against the working conditions of the unskilled laborers employed in the fast food industry, against the religious fundamentalism creeping into the diaspora, against police brutality. It takes me a while to decide which side I am on because inasmuch as these issues on the surface seem like, you know, obvious—yes, racism is terrible, yes, volenece agant this or that is horrible, but few things are as simple as that. By the time I am done with my little research and know for sure, for sure, what I think, the matter becomes passé. So I stick to Zaidi's Urdu society.

Rizwan: Well, that battle is Tausif's.

me: *violence against this or that

Why are you so hell bent on undermining Zaidi's contributions all the freaking time? It's like you hope he didn't exist.

Monday, 24 February 2014
3:30 AM

From: ira.chattrejee12@h-mail.com
To: amberscrawls@h-mail.com

Amby,
I always wrote better at night but now I'm no good for writing at any time of the day. Right now I heard a knock on my door and woke up but there was no one. It is not even Friday or Saturday night for people to prank. I considered dialing 911. *Fasahat* is not here. He left for India two weeks ago and I haven't heard from him since. He is not replying to my e-mails. I don't have his number in India. I have lived alone before and

that doesn't scare me. Someone did knock. Every other time, *Fasahat* at least informs me after he's reached. I am thinking how everyone actually disliked *Fasahat*. Riz, you, my mom. Mom is barely talking to me now that I have told her I don't belong in the global screw and propagate squad. You always worried about what *Fasahat* would do to me. And now he's done it. I opened his closet yesterday. It has those kurtas he wore at the readings, boxes of medicines, and assorted objects: coasters with names scribbled on them, napkins with almost-formed couplets, pebbles from god-knows-where, tickets of concerts and films, cat treats, light bulbs, empty packets of spices and tea, and this sketch of a well within a labyrinth on a scrap of paper. It could be from his childhood, you know. He had written to me about it once. I thought he was making up the story but the sketch is sitting here in his closet.

Then I look at the rest of my apartment. It is an extension of Zaidi's closet. We kept all the stuff that Mike, Xian, and you left behind when you moved. Zaidi was always big on abandoned goods. During our expedition to antique shops, he would pick up weird little objects. Once he bought an empty rusted can of a soup brand that had gone out of business quarter of a century ago for 30 bucks. Now, I come from a family of hoarders. Nothing leaves the threshold of our house in Kolkata. We even have my grandpa's ancient typewriters and fountain pens neatly stored in some box. But the thing about Zaidi that I found remarkable, when I went to antique shops with him, was that he was not only trying to hold on to his or his loved ones' memories but also those of strangers. He keenly accumulated memories that he couldn't have made. I doubt if all the things in his closet are his or he sneaked them from other people, from places he visited.... What kind of a person does that?

Thursday, 27 February 2014
3:00 PM

Babe, for what it's worth, I had no reason to dislike *Fasahat*.
He's entertaining, kind, and we were pals. You got to put a
stopper on your thoughts about him and concentrate on your
work. I'm sure he will get in touch with you. Know that I've
been thinking of you the whole time after Xian and I attended
an exhibition showcasing fiberglass sculptures collected over
the last four decades from artists worldwide. The inaugural
talks were all about the boundaries separating art from craft,
which you lurveee debating!

11:45 PM

from: Rizwan Syed <s.rizwan85@h-mail.com>
to: ira.chatterjee@h-mail.com

Ira,
Nothing is certain but let's prepare ourselves for the worst.
Fasahat met Tausif's cousin at the hospital and told his family
that he'll be in town as long as Tausif does not recover. They
did not see or hear from him for a week. When they called
his house, they learned that he had never even gone there. On
the same day some eyewitnesses saw a young man fall into a
well. This well, Shava Bavli, is in a protected area, a historical
site. There was no splash of water, no sound. Search for him
continues. Tausif's condition is stable now.

Rizwan.

11

Dissolve. Only seconds before the tip of the nose sinks, the nose with a ring or a stud. The frame whirls its way downstream. Boys slide on the river of clay to snatch the buoyant ornaments off the idol. Membranophone beats to keep the time come undone. Ladies and gentlemen, a very good evening. The local time here is 8:43. Air is not silent when ceding way to a ballistic body. We have a moving map display to track our progress. Sometimes they row the pratima midstream before throwing it overboard. Water can not drown sound. The weather today is rather pleasant. The man on her left feels his way through the pocket of the seat in front of him. Are you looking for ear plugs or are you already queasy?

Understated iris wafted from Zaidi's fleece-lined pea coat she sold to a thrift shop. His microphone was always slanted, 45 degrees from the mouth on the horizontal axis, but no phonemes escaped. Paws of a crystal leopard bought off the shelves of an antic mall near Berlin, Ohio, held the pleats of his pallu in place. Four hours delay in Abu Dhabi due to the weather. As soon as her eyelids shut, vignettes break open. Her stomach hurts. In Amber's charcoal strokes, her soft bulges were yielding to the traces of infundibulopelvic ligament when Zaidi burst into the room, accidentally. She reached for the housecoat lying on the floor but her fingers ran into the scratches on its wooden surface. Those were Eliot's doing, on the evening when she came back neutered.

Free WiFi at the airport offers respite. 63 new e-mails in 12 hours. None from Zaidi. Sneha reports that a 25-feet model has been missing from a busy Kolkata crossing since last night. missingpeopleandthings.org.in periodically refreshes on her browser. 8913 people missing this year, so far. But who misses them? And 93 monuments not found. They refuse to count Zaidi among those missing. She looks around. The walls of the airport shine with greetings in nastaliq. These are opaque to her and the words' gold lining is tacky. The dust storm subsides, it always subsides.

Open the window shades for landing. Terminal 3 of Indira Gandhi International Airport. Yes, her face matches the passport photograph clicked when she was in college. She can go ahead and take her baggage from the carousel. Three and a half hours stopover before the flight to Lucknow. This is the final leg of the journey that was overdue. Perhaps written on a slippery road. Perhaps written on the stones of a labyrinth. Too many casualties on the way.

How did Riz find her? Yes, she had written to him about her layover in Delhi. There he is now. In a ruffled cobalt blue shirt with rolled sleeves, adjusting a brown cross-body bag, he approaches her. She has a couple of hours in hand before boarding the next flight. He doesn't. He has to go through the security checks in 15 minutes. His flight to Madurai departs in an hour. These are weeks leading up to the international conference.

Where will she stay in Lucknow?

Looking at Riz today you would not believe that he was the one who had the longest and the most enduring association with Zaidi. He does not even inquire about him. Riz will never understand her and Zaidi's situation. How they lived in that Midwestern la-la-land, Riz will never know. All Riz remembers to remind her are those trite lessons from college where a professor, while closely reading Sylvia Plath's 'The Moon and the Yew Tree', observed that denial is the first stage of mourning. Riz has accepted that Zaidi is not around, that he is missing, hidden from view, lurking somewhere in the thickets, or not. She looks past the annoying tone of Riz's e-mails. Looks past him. That is how he has always been.

But Zaidi is an artist, the kind of artist who opens doors, takes you by the hand, and shows you paths that you did not know existed. He takes you to the pinnacle past the thousand stairs until you see the city anew for what it is, with its ruined minarets. From up there other concerns seem trivial. Whether or not you have happiness, you have everlasting beauty. The dawn that you will never forget, the dance of the miniscule dust particles in the shafts of light or the embossed paisley on the tea pot that you will never miss once you have seen it. What had Zaidi seen in Riz?

When will she return?

To the US? As soon as she finds Zaidi.

No. To Kolkata.

That is not even part of the plan. She does not want to go home. No nerve for the long-promised conversation with Mom. Not right now at least. She will wait for Zaidi unlike Riz who has moved on to other things, taking an absurd piece of information in his stride.

What about her fieldwork?

It was a good thing that she photographed Pratima's first solo sculpture at the intersection last year. Only a few hours ago Sneha e-mailed—the 25-feet model has been uprooted from its pedestal. One of the several models to be removed. The state government has decided to replace those with the statues of freedom fighters. Some students from the city's colleges have come out to protest. But frankly, what more can you expect from bureaucrats and politicians who have no clue about arts or aesthetics?

Had Riz ever seen the sculpture?

Yes, he had. Its sweeping curves on all sides—weren't they threaded like chromosome?

Chromosome?

Yes, that thing in the nucleus of—

She knows the textbook definition of chromosomes but Pratima's sculpture was no DNA diagram. Could Pratima ever have seen a DNA diagram? Well, for that matter, could Pratima have imagined DNA diagrams?

That's how Riz saw it. He can not unsee what he has seen.

What about the hole in the middle? What did Riz think of it? Pratima said it was nothing but wasn't it a well?

There is nothing in Lucknow, Riz interjects. It was exactly what he had been writing to her all these months anyway. He would explode if he had to repeat those words one more time. So, Ira blurted out the supposition that she had let only half form in the fear of what it could possibly entail, could she have found Zaidi, in Lucknow, *ever*?

This was Ira demanding answers as she always did, convinced that she had a right to them. Riz knew this movement of eyes and this inflection in her voice but today it was without the candour that angered and amused him by turns. Riz wondered how Fatima, whom he had known for what now seemed like the brisk pause ensuing as one's eyes move from one line of verse to another, would have answered that question. Sometimes he goes looking for Fatima in the

poems he had once collected, even as he knows that she does
not want anyone, least of all him, to find her. She wanted him
to hold Fasahat. And it will always be Fatima *or* Fasahat, he
knew. Did Fasahat never tell Ira the stonemason's story? And
then he saw. This woman in front of him was not expecting
answers from him, not today. Perhaps, he could ask something
of her. So, tentatively he does: What about Pratima? Where
is she now?

Ira had been here previously, aboard a tram, years back. The
red bricks of this old colonial mansion look over a green lake.
A young girl strikes two stones and sings a kitschy Bangla
song, asks for money. A boy carries a tray full of chewing
gum and salted peanuts enclosed in transparent plastic
wrappers. Snacks to eat while you wait for the bus on your
way back from the office. The red private buses with yellow
stripes whiz past in the street. Ticket, ticket, ticket. Vans from
media houses have found permanent spots on either side of
this building, which has the faces of three lions stamped
on its forehead. Today a restless group has gathered under
the auspices of the building. From a crow's eye-view this is
a small but determined congregation. How long will their
slogans demanding a sculpture back last?
       The bells had rung for the lunch break on an autumnal
afternoon like this. Some athletes from the college team were
dribbling a basketball near the backcourt of the compound.
Ashwin slung the guitar on his shoulders, Riz got hold of
cymbals from somewhere, and Ira stood with a black cloth
tied around her eyes. That was her part. They would perform
a play on this uneven ground. The play was in couplets. There
would be music to lift the rhythm. It was the four of them.
At first. The gathered crowd soon drowned the guitar and

the cymbals with claps and snapping fingers. The action mounted, as streams of sweat made their way to the ground in silence. The college's vice-principal broke the group apart. By the time they graduated, she forgot that moment when, despite being blindfolded, she saw most vividly.

When Pratima first heard of the missing sculpture she was staggered. Years of her life had been held together in that abstract plaster form. It was milk white when she had carved it. When they came to take it away from the studio, the sculpture was tied in red ribbons. Some powerful person cut the ribbon. A plaque spelt out the name of her daughter in larger font and her name in a smaller font right below it. She folded her hands in acknowledgement when they handed her a bouquet of flowers. The end of her sari was caught in a nail, stubbornly jutting out from the hastily erected makeshift wooden stage by the corner of the street next to the sculpture. She managed to reach the designated white chair, without tripping, with her daughter next to her. The chief guest's voice, amplified by the loudspeaker, was emphasizing the need to beautify the city. It is not only the responsibility of the government to promote works of art but also the citizens' to maintain it. He mentioned how on his recent trip to Singapore he found out that even Indians don't spit on the roads there. From Singapore he soon reached America where monuments like the Statue of Liberty have been installed and conserved. She could no longer attend to what this man was saying about countries to which she had never been. Instead she followed the rise and fall of the traffic's noise. The cars were moving slow, annoyed for having to leave half the street to some random ongoing event at this busy hour. Cycles and rickshaws were trying to squeeze in between the cars. Soon a middle-aged man sitting in the last row among the audience started shouting at a rickshaw puller. The rickshaw's wheels had grazed his chair. Can't he see? Is he trying to kill people early in the morning? Does he think he's piloting a jet? When she returned to the chief speaker, he was almost done. In conclusion, he said, we ought to protect the interests of the city and keep it clean. Protect the interests of the artists and enable them to present their rich work and heritage. No better site than the intersection of Belaghata and bypass. Delegates from all over the world take the bypass after they land at the airport. Indeed she has been granted a privilege of which other artists merely dream. So when the sculpture was removed, she concluded that the dream was over. The faces of the idols that she had once chiselled had dissolved. This sculpture was anyway gathering dust on a street. Perhaps nobody ever turned to look at it. She did not know that she wanted this sculpture reinstated. But then she thought of her.

Ira had spent months looking for her. She had meant to recover her and thought she had succeeded. There was nothing more to be done. She had her own idol—the one she had managed to sculpt. But the well into which idols plummet had been dug. For months she dreamt of walking amid mirrors surrounding that well with her forefingers hooked to a string of powdered glass. Yet there was nowhere to go. Now there are only questions to be answered at home. And elsewhere. Everywhere. Long days ahead. Making her way through the crowd in front of the red building, Ira finds her. Through the descending evening, she sits beside her, recuperating from the tortuous journey, demanding the missing be restored, as soon as possible, and waiting for someone to collect her stories.

Epilogue

The Collected Poems and Translations
with select correspondences
[2011-2014]
Fasahat Zaidi

Compiled by
Ira Chatterjee

Delhi
Spring Home Press
San Francisco Kolkata Lucknow
2015

Acknowledgements

Ma and Baba taught me to love Lucknow and Kolkata but this novel owes its life to the artists of Kumartuli. Shyamal Paul, Gopal Chandra Paul, Jyotindranath Paul, Sunil Paul, Sanatan Paul, Badal Paul, Subol Paul, and Sridam Paul told me their stories even before I knew what I would do with them. Turns out stories ask to be told and retold.

An extract from this novel was first published in *Himal Southasian* (http://himalmag.com) on 7 April 2015, and I appreciate Elen Turner's insightful comments on that manuscript. The extract has been reprinted here with permission.

My friend and first reader, Narmada, deserves commendation for ploughing through a very rough draft and my partner, Rajat, for successfully distracting me from writing, when I needed it. Finally, I am grateful to Arpita for sharing my vision for this novel and the many discussions we have had about it.

Publisher's Note

The book uses both American and British spelling in keeping with the differing formats used in it. For instance, the emails follow American spelling while the narrative in the voice of the Kumartuli artist follows British spelling. This distinction has been maintained to convey the disparateness of form.

Made in the USA
San Bernardino, CA
17 January 2019